THE WHISPERING DEAD OF REWLEY ABBEY

DR. PETER STEPHENSON

HISTORIUM PRESS

HISTORIUM PRESS

To Deborah,
my late wife and devoted partner of 50 years.
I am sad that you never got to see this dream come to
fruition.

Table of Contents

Dramatis Personae

Introduction

Chapter 18: Burden of Truth

- In which Sister Agnes struggles with the growing danger of her pursuit and we see the killer's unraveling mental state as clues begin to align against him.

Chapter 19: Beneath the Moon's Gaze

- In which we observe a suspenseful encounter between Sister Agnes and the killer, though his identity remains veiled.

Chapter 20: The Crumbling Veil

- In which we see Sister Agnes and Lady Beatrix solving the Riddle of the Song, anticipating another murder, and closing in on the killer's identity which, when revealed, leads to a confrontation during which the killer is captured. Deceit from an unexpected quarter is revealed.

Chapter 21: Trial of Shadows

- In which we observe the confession of Isabel and the killer's trial.

Chapter 22: The Chilling Eve

- In which a chilling discovery after evening prayers leads Sister Agnes to question the extent of malevolent forces at play as she uncovers a missing fragment of a manuscript, hinting at sinister undercurrents that may threaten the peace of Godstow Abbey.

Historical Notes

Acknowledgements

Preview: Book 2 of the *Sister Agnes and Lady Beatrix Mysteries – The Witch of Godstow Abbey*

Dramatis Personae

Thomas of Hereford

Thomas is a newly minted lecturer at Balliol College of the University of Oxford. Newly minted, perhaps, but with great promise, Thomas rapidly is ascending to the academic heights of the college.

Sir Willam of Hereford

Sir Willam is Thomas' father. He makes no bones about his disapproval of his son's academic aspirations.

Brother Ambrose

Brother Ambrose is a Cistercian monk, living at Rewley Abbey. He is a former instructor of Thomas and now a close friend.

Lady Elinore de Beauchamp

Gibert's mother and the wife of Edmund. Lady Elinore is from a noble family beset by hard times. She married Edmund for financial security.

Gilbert of Shrewsbury

Gilbert has mysterious intentions. He is a troubled, jealous young man, inflamed by his younger sister's "golden child" position in the family. He fluctuates between feeling himself powerful and falling into violent rage.

Edmund of Shrewsbury

Gilbert's father, a very successful merchant, rising from the status of peddler to the owner of a successful butcher shop. He has groomed Gilbert's younger sister to take over the business at his death.

Isabella

Isabella is the younger sister of Gilbert.

Isabel de Beauchamp

Isabel is a young novice at Godstow Abbey, home of Benedictine nuns. She works in the infirmary under Sister Agnes. She aspires to take her final vows and become Sister Catherine.

Sister Agnes

Sister Agnes is a Benedictine nun living at Godstow Abbey. She is the abbey's infirmarist, supervising the activities of the abbey's infirmary. She is an accomplished healer, herbalist, nurse and anatomist. She becomes involved with solving the crime of murder.

Mother Superior (see Mother Alice de Gorges below)

Mother Superior is the Abbess at Godstow Abbey. She is struggling with developing a good working relationship with Sister Agnes.

Lady Beatrix de Aylesbridge

Lady Beatrix and her noble family are benefactors of Godstow Abbey. She has developed a close friendship with Sister Agnes and will assist her in solving crimes.

Mateld

Mateld is a young barmaid at the Black Swan Inn. She is the recipient of unwanted attention from Gilbert, and she fights back injuring him.

The Confessor

The Confessor is an elderly priest who hears the confessions of the nuns at Godstow Abbey.

Lady Rosamunde

Lady Rosamunde – "The Fair Rosamunde" – is an historical figure, mistress to King Henry II, and buried at Godstow. She appears in a recurring dream by the young novice Isabella.

Undersheriff, Alric the Bald

The sheriff, Henry de Thisteldon, is the chief law enforcement officer in Oxfordshire and was a real person. Alric is the undersheriff reporting directly to the sheriff and carrying out most of the local investigations while Sheriff de Thisteldon attends to administrative tasks. Alric is a fictional character.

Proctor Cedric Stonehand

The proctor is an official of the University of Oxford, responsible for upholding its statutes and maintaining order among students. Proctor Stonehand is part of Balliol College.

Deputy Coroner Adam de Wallingford

The coroner is an official appointed to investigate deaths of a suspicious or sudden nature, ensuring they are properly recorded and justice is sought in Oxfordshire. The actual coroner of the time was Adam de Spalding, coroner of Oxford town. The fictional, Adam de Wallingford is his deputy.

Wystan the Sage

A mystic and master of dark magic and the occult arts. The killer consults him regarding his recurring nightmare of the murder.

Eric du Nordsk

A knight Templar whose father was a Viking warrior, come to England with other raiders. He married an Englishwoman of French heritage.

Mother Alice de Gorges

Mother Alice is the prioress/mother superior of Godstow Abbey. She was a real person who served from 1295 until her death in 1304.

Alexis, Bard of the Shire

Alexis is an Irish Celtic bard and seer. She wanders Oxfordshire with her family including her maternal grandmother who also is a seer. She prophesies through her songs and stories. Alexis is inspired by a real person, at the time of this writing, a young singer/songwriter.

Professor Reginald Barrington

Professor Barrington is a lifelong academic, educated at Baliol College and a noted world traveler and scholar. His specialty areas are civil and ecclesiastical law, expert on heresy and church law and an interpreter of heretical symbols and texts. He is sought out by Sister Agnes and Lady Beatrix as an advisor in his areas of expertise.

PROLOG

IN THE SPRING of 1295, the unusually warm, dry spring of Trinity Term at Oxford University heralded an impending hot, arid summer. The minds of students and dons turned toward the welcome respite of the upcoming break at end of term.

But that was not to be.

Before the onset of the next academic cycle with the Michaelmas Term, the dirt streets of Oxford Town would be abuzz with whispers of a vicious murder just outside the stoic walls of nearby Rewley Abbey. The tragedy would cast a shadow over Balliol College, robbing it of a promising academic. The motive? Obscure. Suspects? None.

Local taverns and inns soon filled with speculations. The unwelcome heat of this unusual spring fuelled restlessness among the people of Oxford. By the time the coroner's inquest reached its crescendo, the townsfolk, driven by whispers and rumours, had their theories. Every theory, it seemed, except a valid one.

The crime posed relentless questions. Why near Rewley? Was the malevolent hand behind the deed clad in the austere robe of a Cistercian monk? Or was it a student, given that Oxford's history was, unfortunately, punctuated with unsolved student-related homicides? Had the victim, a lecturer, inadvertently incited his own demise?

Murders during this era often stemmed from persistent human vices: greed, envy, or perhaps one too many steins of the strong, local ale. Love spats, town-gown disputes, or simmering feuds usually had transparent culprits. Yet, the spring of 1295 seemed to provide at least one ample exception. Still more questions.

Why, for example, did the Master of Balliol College exhibit such unwavering aggression to unmask the killer? The victim's bereaved parents were, of course, clamouring for justice, but their fervour seemed excessively intense. And why was the victim at Rewley Abbey? Might a monk be involved?

As the season's warmth intensified, the townsfolk's speculations, exacerbated by the unseasonable weather, seemed only to jumble the investigation further. The local sheriff and Balliol Proctor, bereft of any substantial leads, were drowning in a quagmire of uncertainty, confusion, and frustration.

Then, from the sidelines, emerged an improbable pair of sleuths, seeking to unravel this tapestry of mystery. Sister Agnes, a Benedictine nun, and her high-born friend and sometimes collaborator Lady Beatrix sought the killer using forensic techniques beyond the times. Could these two surprising investigators solve the crime when the sheriff and his minions could not?

Therein lies our tale.

CHAPTER I: A SCHOLAR'S AMBITION

In which we are introduced to Thomas of Hereford and the scholastic atmosphere of Oxford

THOUGH THE WARM. spring afternoon in Oxford bathed the streets in a bright, sunny light, unknown to Lecturer Thomas of Hereford, it masked a shadow of finality. No lectures awaited him today, no disputations, no student meetings — a rare hiatus he intended to cherish. As he stepped out of his rooms at Balliol College into the bright sunlight, revelling in the promise of tranquillity, little did he realize this Trinity term would be his last.

Life as an Oxford lecturer was a privileged one. Especially privileged for a 24-year-old son of one of the oldest houses of nobility in Oxfordshire. Being of the House of Hereford meant money, respect, and the keys to wherever he wanted to go in life. Tall, slim, and with dark, close-cropped hair, Thomas projected the ascetic image of a young academic, especially in his dark academic gown.

When he asserted that he was pursuing a faculty position at Balliol College in the university, his father, clearly disappointed, insisted that young Thomas do something a bit more typical of his class. But Thomas was adamant and his father ultimately had naught to do but go along.

Thomas recalled the confrontation with his father well – almost verbatim. Sir Willam was a stern man who insisted on obedience and having his own way. For this meeting, he clearly wanted to intimidate his son. Dressed in a formal tunic, and dark mantle adorned with the symbols of his knighthood, a bejewelled ceremonial dagger at his belt and his signet ring, Sir Willam was the picture of a rigid, stern military officer.

"There is no benefit to you following this path, Thomas. Certainly, you must have an education, but becoming a lowly teacher? It is beneath you." He brought his fist down hard on the large oak desk. "I forbid it!"

Thomas faced down his father looking him square in the eye. "I have no intention of becoming a lazy, lie-about landed gentleman of the manor. I intend to do something useful with my life, and that is an end of it."

"I certainly could disinherit you, you know."

"Then do as you will. I'm going back to Balliol." And Thomas stormed out of the high-ceilinged library in Hereford Manor slamming the massive door behind him. Neither he nor Sir Willam realized that it was the last meeting they ever would have.

The library door slammed with a resounding echo, and left Sir Willam alone amidst towering shelves of ancient texts, his personal symbols of authority—small shield here, relics of his order of knighthood there—and whispering shadows. He sank into his heavy, overstuffed leather chair, the severity of his stern expression softening into a mix of worry and resignation as he stared at the closed door. The room stifled around him, the weight of words, spoken and unspoken, hanging heavily in the still, dusty air.

Thomas stormed through the manor's corridors lined with the ghost-like portraits of Hereford ancestors, his heart pounding in his chest; a mixture of indignation and a strange sense of liberation coursed through his veins. But along with it, a faint sting of regret gnawed at him, for he cherished the bond with his father despite their disagreements.

As he stepped out into the warm, still air, he could not

help but wonder about the widening gulf between them, the uncertain currents of the future swirling ominously in his mind. Was this a harbinger of things to come? Thomas drove the thought from his mind and turned back toward Balliol College.

Thomas at Balliol

Young Thomas was admitted as a fellow at Balliol College, one of Oxford's oldest institutions, to pursue his advanced studies. He demonstrated remarkable aptitude in the liberal arts, mastering the disciplines of the Trivium—grammar, logic, and rhetoric—and becoming increasingly adept in Latin, the language of scholarly discourse. His academic endeavours continued with distinction in the Quadrivium— arithmetic, geometry, music, and astronomy marking him as a scholar of considerable promise. It was not long before Balliol's Master called Thomas to his chambers, a potentially frightening event.

The Master was imposing in his robe, hood, cap, and large signet ring used for sealing official documents.

"Thomas, you are one of the most exceptional students Balliol has seen in many a long year. Your rapid assimilation not only of subject matter—which we expect of our scholars—has been significantly augmented by your obvious comfort in the academic environment, here at Balliol"

"Thank you, sir. I quite enjoy the academic life."

"I want you to think about something, Thomas."

"Sir?"

"How would you like to stay on after graduation, work

on your master's and take a post as a lecturer?"

"I would very much like that, sir. A career in academia, especially here at Balliol would serve me well."

"Then it is settled. I'll have my provost draft the proper paperwork, and you go ahead and enrol for your master's."

And so, Thomas went on to complete his bachelor studies with high honours and embarked on his master's studies, teaching logic and philosophy as a lecturer along the way. He chose a quiet life of contemplation and study when he was not lecturing. He had few friends and led a rather introspective existence questioning the philosophies of the day and the teachings of the Church.

One of those few friends, however, and a fairly close one at that, was Brother Ambrose, a Cistercian monk from the nearby monastery at Rewley Abbey. A teacher of Philosophy at Balliol, Brother Ambrose became acquainted with Thomas during the course of Thomas' studies under him at the college. Thomas was extraordinarily brilliant, and it was not long until a friendship with Brother Ambrose developed. It was not uncommon for Thomas to find time to visit the monk at Rewley Abbey and engage in in-depth discussions on philosophical and theological topics, interpreting classical and contemporary texts, debating the moral, metaphysical, and epistemological issues of the day.

Thomas at the Abbey

Thomas left the college, passed the town wall, and wandered aimlessly along Broad Street and on to Cornmarket Street. The stately presence of St. Martin's Church at Carfax commanded his attention, with its prominent tower standing as a testament to Oxford's growth.

As he continued his journey, the imposing Oxford Castle soon loomed before him. Constructed by Robert D'Oyly after the Norman Conquest, it had grown from its early wooden fortifications to the stone structure that now stood before him. It was rumoured that D'Oyly built the castle as much to protect himself from attacks from outside its massive stone walls as to protect the town from attacks from within.

As he ventured further, the bustling sounds and pungent aromas from the marketplace momentarily overwhelmed him. Eager for respite, he left the town and wandered along the banks of the River Isis until he found himself at the tranquil grounds of Rewley Abbey, the sanctuary of his friend, Brother Ambrose.

He found the monk in the chapel, and they retired to the quiet of the garden, a serene haven within the monastic walls, for discussion and quiet contemplation. Dressed in the unique white tunic, scapular, rosary, and cowl, Brother Ambrose was the picture of a Cistercian monk. The tranquil atmosphere was punctuated only by the singing of the birds and the distant chants of monks practising for the evening Vespers. After a time, Brother Ambrose broke the silence.

"What think you, Thomas, of the decrees from the Second Council of Lyon under Pope Gregory?"

"We have debated this many times before, Brother Ambrose. It calls for further crusades against the Saracens, presumably to reclaim Jerusalem and our sacred sites. Must we continually shed blood in the name of our faith? Is it not enough to live in peace and let others do the same? Besides, Gregory has been dead these many years. Boniface is now Pope."

"Ah, yes, Thomas, but each time, as you study and contemplate, your position wavers. Do you not see the spiritual importance of reclaiming those sacred places for Christendom? Boniface, too, supports the crusades. He continues in the tradition under Gregory."

"I'm sorry, Brother Ambrose, but you will never persuade me that blood must be shed to dominate a piece of land. Lives are always more important than conquest for territory. Now I really must go. Vespers are soon, and I must prepare a lecture for the morrow."

"It always is good to contemplate the world and the Church with you, Thomas. I am uneasy with your stance on this matter; however, but it is your position. Though I urge you to continue mulling over the issues, I can do no more than try to present persuasive arguments in its favour."

And with that, Thomas left the abbey garden, his mind burdened by the brief, yet intense debate, and started the walk back to his rooms at Balliol.

Thomas - The Long Walk Back

Brother Ambrose had not, exactly, chastised Thomas for his views on the Crusades. However, the debate left Thomas troubled. As he slowly approached the castle, a small troop of Knights Templar rode past. They bore the Beauceant battle banners - a black section above white with the iconic red cross. Their glistening white shields also bore the prominent red crosses, and their armour glowed red in the setting sun. The moment was not lost on Thomas.

For centuries, since the earliest days of the Crusades, whispers persisted of a large manor house near the Templar outpost at Sandford Preceptory. While this preceptory was one of the most significant in England, the manor house nearby was rumoured to be a place of safekeeping for Templar treasure. Thomas's mind fleetingly dwelt on the myths of Templar treasures, but his deeper contemplations still focused on his confrontation with Brother Ambrose. The sight of this small troop of knights only accentuated the sharpness of his memory and the slight pain from the tone the debate with his friend had taken.

Rapidly reversing his earlier stroll to the abbey, Thomas approached St. Martin's Church. In the shadowy recesses of Oxford's history, whispered tales told of an underground passage connecting the Sandford Preceptory and the nearby manor house to St. Martin's Church, and, perhaps, to Rewley Abbey. This secretive tunnel was rumoured to have been used by Templars when they needed to convene discreetly with religious and civic leaders in the heart of Oxford, away from prying eyes.

Over the years, as the church's foundations weakened and renovations took place, the entrance to this passage was lost to time and new construction. However, local lore persisted that within the confines of the church, particularly somewhere within or beneath the tower of St. Martin's church, there lay an entrance to the hidden Templar passageway.

These tales grew especially vivid as the Templars' reputation in Oxfordshire grew to include secreting of treasure and important documents. More rumours spread that in those tumultuous days, select Templars used this passage to transport and hide treasures, artefacts, and documents of immense importance, entrusting them to the care of Oxford's clergy. *Including Brother Ambrose, perhaps?* Some even believed that these treasures still lay hidden somewhere beneath the streets of Oxford, or perhaps, in the manor house nearby, awaiting discovery.

Thomas could not erase these images from his mind. As a leading figure in the Cistercian order, St. Bernard of Clairvaux had been instrumental in promoting and endorsing the Templar order. His treatise, *In Praise of the New Order of Knighthood,* provided a powerful theological justification for Christian knighthood.

Though written centuries before, it remained influential, reminding many of the original ideals and spiritual fervour that had driven the earlier Crusades. *Could Brother Ambrose be in some way involved in a conspiracy to renew the Crusades or seek the mythical treasure?* While Brother Ambrose certainly was not on the battle side of the Crusades, he clearly could be providing spiritual endorsement to the Knights or, more materially, he could have participated in secreting, or, more likely, seeking the Templar treasure.

Thomas shoved these thoughts from his mind. Certainly, the stories of the Templars in Oxfordshire were naught but myths and legends.

Certainly.

Without really realizing it, Thomas found himself back at Balliol. Though it was spring, the sun still set somewhat early, and the skies took on a reddish glow as the sun set over Wytham Hill. Vespers were not far off and, eschewing his lecture preparations, Thomas decided to go directly to the chapel.

Thomas turned rapidly towards the college's chapel, his thoughts still swirling from his afternoon's travels. He sought the peace and tranquillity of the chapel and the comforting end of his academic day in the company of the Balliol community, and the choir with its calming, even hypnotic, Gregorian chants.

As he approached the chapel, he noted someone that he thought that he had seen before walking stealthily behind a building several yards away. He put the thought away and entered the chapel.

Thomas did not know it, but he had glimpsed, however vaguely, his executioner.

CHAPTER 2: ENVIOUS SHADOWS

In which we are introduced to Gilbert of Shrewsbury and his growing animosity towards Thomas and others

Gilbert of Shrewsbury lounged in the Black Swan tavern. Mateld, the pert, loquacious bar maid prattled on about something. Gilbert barely heard her.

"Another pint of ale, Mateld, and don't dawdle!"

"Coming Master Gilbert. Coming," she replied in overworked frustration. She pulled a pint, delivered the ale, and flounced off, her drab green kirtle ruffling in the breeze of her rapid departure. Her apron swished back and forth about her knees.

Well into his third pint of the strong local ale, Gilbert contemplated the young barmaid. Certainly, younger than he—perhaps as much as five years less than his 28—she was, if not particularly pretty... surely, handsome. He would have to give a bit of consideration to Mateld. Yes, indeed he would. She might make a tasty little morsel one of these nights.

The night cooled as the warming sun set below the horizon. Gilbert took another draught of his ale and shivered involuntarily. He got up from his stool at the bar and walked unsteadily over to claim a chair by the large, roaring fire. That surely would take his chill away. Something else, he thought, might also take his chill away: Mateld.

He quickly downed the dregs of his ale and called for the barmaid.

"Mateld! Another ale."

She arrived a moment or so later, but before she could set the mug down, Gilbert grabbed her around her waist and pulled her into his lap.

"C'mon, lass. Let me show you what a real man is like."

Mateld pulled her arm behind her, still holding the mug of ale, and with a broad swing like a bare-knuckle fighter, she slapped him across his face with the mug, and dropped it on the table in front of him. Gilbert's eyes widened with pain and surprise, but before he could retaliate, the ale he drunk earlier caught up with him, dizzying him. In a split second, Mateld fled.

Moments later, Gilbert nursed his face and took another swig of what was left of the ale. The landlord, a brawny brute of a man, wiped his hands on his leather apron, and walked up to Gilbert.

"Tis the end of you for the night, m'lad. Get up and get out of here 'fore I send for the sheriff. And if you ever do that again, ye'll wake up in the gaol."

Gilbert dragged himself to his feet and sloughed to the door. The others in the room called out after him, hooting, laughing, and mocking.

"The maid bested you; did she not?"

"Think she'll go yer bail next time, laddie?" from a gruff old Scotsman sitting at the bar.

"Haply, she'll tek ye there herself!" guffaw from the rest of the patrons.

But Gilbert was gone.

Gilbert – Quiet Contemplation and a Hangover

Gilbert, weary and inebriated, walked slowly back to his

cramped quarters in St. Giles Hall at Balliol, a space he begrudgingly shared with another student. Fortunately, his room mate was absent, likely attending Vespers or some other religious service that held no appeal for Gilbert that night. Pain throbbed in his head, and his face, sore from Mateld's blow, was beginning to swell. As he removed his tunic for bed, the room spun, echoing the turmoil of his thoughts.

While Gilbert typically was not one for introspection, favouring the tangible over the reflective, that evening he felt an undeniable disruption in his life. Naturally, he didn't consider himself at fault—it was never his doing. However, amidst his haziness, he contemplated delving into the root of his current misery. *Surely, he wasn't the problem. Perhaps, it was merely the ale's influence.* Yet, in this clouded state, he decided to assess his circumstances and the misfortunes others had seemingly imposed upon him. And then, he would exact his revenge.

Foremost among his perceived adversaries was his father, Edmund of Shrewsbury. Edmund was a renowned shopkeeper in Oxford. Having graduated from a market stall to owning a butcher shop, his shrewd decisions and honest dealings established his notable success. Gilbert reflected on how his father, diligent and committed, embodied the adage, "the proof of the pudding is in the eating." Yet, Edmund's relentless push for Gilbert to emulate him only fueled Gilbert's resentment.

Gilbert's thoughts then drifted to his mother, the once-high-born Lady Elinor, daughter of a diminished nobility. Despite the fall from grace, she retained her refined demeanour, a trait that complemented his father's upward growth from a simple stall keeper to a wealthy and respected businessman. While they did not quite belong to the nobility, Gilbert's parents had secured a place of respect within Oxford's business circles and even received occasional nods from neighbouring noble families. This increasingly grated on Gilbert.

Lady Elinor's dowry had primarily consisted of lands. With her family's dwindling fortunes—a situation not uncommon among lesser nobility—the upkeep of these lands proved burdensome. Eventually, they were sold off. In Gilbert's eyes, his mother was a pretender. Though birthed into the nobility, she had lost any genuine, noble claim.

And then there was Isabella, his younger sister, the apple of his father's eye. She was being groomed as the successor to the family business. It was not that Gilbert desired that responsibility, but the mere idea that a young girl would inherit it all felt wrong. After all, he was the elder and the male heir. By rights, the legacy was his. Even if he had no interest in maintaining it, he could always sell the business and enjoy the profits.

Engulfed by the perceived injustices his family dealt him, Gilbert's disordered thoughts shifted elsewhere. Perhaps prompted by the throbbing in his jaw, he settled first on young women like Mateld, who, in his opinion, held themselves in unreasonably high esteem. He silently vowed that he'd soon put Mateld in her place.

His thoughts then wandered to his peers at the college. A bitterness stirred within him against those fellow students at Balliol, younger, yet more academically accomplished. While he had indeed carved a name for himself at the college, it was tied to tales of debauchery, dalliances, and wild revelry.

He imagined confronting these self-righteous scholars, dismissing them as effortlessly as swatting away flies in a stifling stable. Some of these upstarts even had obtained positions lecturing at the college. Gilbert could not tolerate the insult that leaving him behind meted out. They, too, would pay.

Tiring, his mind still swirling from Mateld's attack and the local ale, Gilbert finally fell into a restless sleep filled with the jeers from the men in the tavern, and the social activities of his family where nobody seemed to know he was there.

Deep sleep came slowly, but, finally, it came, and Gilbert did not awake until sunrise, the bright sunlight filtering through the small window of his room.

Gilbert – Revenge Begins

Another night at a tavern had ended for Gilbert, though not at the *Black Swan*; his drunken attack on Mateld had made him unwelcome there. As he left *The White Hart*, he spotted Mateld departing for the night from the *Black Swan*, starting on her lengthy journey home. Two hours past the curfew bell's tolling at dusk, they were the lone figures navigating the unlit streets.

Gilbert trailed behind, hiding in the deeper shadows. They moved through Cornmarket Street and then onto High Street, passing by *The Chequers* tavern. Unseen by Mateld, Gilbert loomed ominously behind. As they veered into Alfred Street, where the scant light made the night murkier, Gilbert saw his opportunity. Picking up a stone lying nearby, he tiptoed behind her. Gripping her shoulder, he spun her around to face him.

"Do you recognize me, m'lass? Seems you're due for a lesson after last night."

He swung the stone towards her head. Mateld swerved,

and although she evaded the full force of his blow, the stone still grazed her jaw, causing her to stumble to the ground, dazed but conscious. Gilbert tore the apron from her waist and flung it over her head, covering her face.

"See if you can recognize me now, lass! Spin any tale you like," he hissed, "but if my name crosses your lips, it'll be our last meeting."

Gilbert vanished into the night, leaving Mateld stunned and frightened on the ground.

Gilbert – Back at the College

Triumphant after his attack on Mateld, Gilbert hummed a tune, and walked with a buoyant spring in his step. The streets of Oxford felt brighter, the night air crisper, and every sound more melodic. He was satisfied, not with his possible damage to Mateld, but with his elation of meeting his goal of showing her who he was. It wasn't so much what he did, he thought. It was the thrill of having done it.

It was a long walk from where he confronted Mateld to Balliol and his room at St. Giles Hall, but Gilbert savoured every mile, living his triumph over and over. As he neared St. Giles, he hoped to find some fellow students in the communal room. Though the chances of finding ale were slim due to the hall's strict rules, tonight he felt he could charm even the driest of fountains to spout liquid.

His recent actions, far from weighing on him, instead gave him a boost, a feeling of completion and satisfaction. The darker facets of his nature, usually lurking in the shadows, were beginning to find the light.

The real Gilbert was almost home.

Gilbert – The Other Gilbert

Waking in the bright rays of the spring morning, Gilbert felt transformed from the previous night. The triumphant afterglow of his encounter with Mateld dimmed, replaced by a heady sense of potency. Today, he felt as if he stood atop the world, ready to dominate whatever challenge lay ahead.

He noticed his room mate's absence, assuming he had ventured out for breakfast or perhaps the Prime services in the chapel. However, it was not long before the door swung open, admitting both his room mate and the town's sheriff.

"Where were you after the curfew bell last evening?" the undersheriff demanded without preamble.

"I was at the *White Hart*," Gilbert replied coolly, meeting the undersheriff's gaze without flinching. "After closing, I returned here and stayed the night."

"The young barmaid from the *Black Swan* was found brutally injured," the undersheriff countered, his eyes narrowing. "Though she didn't name you, word has it she crossed paths with you not long ago. Any thoughts?"

A sneer crept onto Gilbert's face. "Unless you can show some evidence tying me to this incident, I suggest you leave. I have prayers to attend."

The unyielding confidence in Gilbert's posture and tone forced the sheriff to reconsider momentarily. Without another word, the lawman turned sharply and left. Gilbert watched him go, the corners of his lips curling into a smug grin.

"Better luck next time, Sheriff," he murmured, revelling in his perceived victory.

Gilbert – More Introspection

After the undersheriff's abrupt departure, Gilbert sank into his austere, straight-backed study chair. A lingering unease gnawed at him. The undersheriff's visit had not been a casual one, it bore an accusatory tone, as if the lawman had suspicions he had yet to voice. Gilbert's lectures beckoned, but he found himself lacking the will to attend, though he knew that he would suffer from this ignoring of the academic rules.

The more he reflected upon recent events, the stronger his conviction grew that he was isolated in this world. There was an itch to act, to reclaim some semblance of control. His own audacity in the face of the sheriff's probing surprised him. That undersheriff had the authority to imprison him or, at worst, condemn him for assaulting Mateld. *Why, then, had he been allowed to walk free?*

His gaze drifted toward the window, his thoughts consumed by a haze, not of slumber but of a daydream-like trance. He pondered over the lost chance with Mateld. Regret started to seep in, but she was the architect of their confrontation, after all. *Hadn't she been the one to strike first, leading him to be the laughingstock of the tavern's regulars?* No. There was nothing to regret on that score.

His thoughts then strayed to other betrayals. His mother, his sister—the root of his torments always seemed to intertwined with the whims of women. The burgeoning anger in him sketched a dark picture: *if they were gone, the pain would cease.* The students who looked through him, the ones who scaled greater academic heights while he stumbled, their dismissiveness was a wound, as well. In his mind, they, along with his lecturers, were the real villains. And with every passing thought, his anger intensified.

Shaking off his reverie, Gilbert ambled into the bustling town centre. As he passed the town's walls, memories of his father's shop surfaced. He promptly dismissed the idea of visiting, his feet instinctively guiding him toward *The White Hart.*

No! On this day, he would return to the *Black Swan* and confront the ones who mocked him. No bar wench would cause him humiliation without a response from him. He would show them all who he was. As he approached the tavern, the landlord met him at the door.

"You're not welcome here, laddie."

CHAPTER 3: THE LAST LECTURE

In which we attend Thomas's final lecture and observe the appearance of a strange message summoning him to a clandestine meeting.

Thomas was in the fragrant garden of Rewley Abbey, deep in conversation with Brother Ambrose, as had become their frequent ritual.

"I've been chosen to deliver the Trinity Lecture at St. Mary's next week, Brother Ambrose."

Brother Ambrose's eyes lit up with a mix of pride and enthusiasm. "What an immense honour, Thomas!"

"It was the master at the college who nominated me. I am contemplating the topic: *The Confluence of Aristotelian Logic with Christian Theology: Pathways to Greater Understanding or Roads to Heresy?*"

Brother Ambrose stroked his beard, thoughtfully. "A challenging yet rewarding topic. May I offer some guidance?"

Thomas nodded, appreciative. "Always. Your insights have never pointed me in the wrong direction, and as you say, it is quite challenging. I must not be seen as promoting *roads to heresy.*"

Brother Ambrose began, "Then I would advise beginning with a reflection on *The Rule of St. Benedict*. It solidly anchors your position within the roots of the Church's teachings and, therefore, invokes the roots of Christianity.

Once that foundation is laid, you then can evoke Aristotle's wisdom. This progression demonstrates that you are inviting intellectual exploration rather than inciting defensive reactions.

From there, delicately traverse the fine line between our core tenets and the enlightenments proffered by Aristotelian logic. Highlight the concerns, particularly the potential drift from the Church's essence, and finally, argue for harmonious integration."

With evident respect, Thomas wove in Brother Ambrose's suggestions, "The Rule commences by stating, He who hears My words and follows them, I will liken him to a wise man who constructed his dwelling upon sturdy rock. From his teachings, could we say that St. Benedict encourages us to be wise?"

Brother Ambrose nodded, prompting Thomas to continue. "While those words set our journey's course, St. Benedict adds depth. He says, 'It is high time for us to arise from sleep'. This will be as a call to those listening to the lecture to heed St. Benedict's words. He also says, 'Is there anyone here who yearns for life and desires to see good days? If you hear this and your answer is "I do," God then directs these words to you: 'If you desire true and eternal life, keep your tongue free from vicious talk and your lips from all deceit; turn away from evil and do good; let peace be your quest and aim.' "

Ambrose smiled. "My son, you have grasped the true meaning of "The Rule". This is the message your lecture must convey: seek eternal life and follow his "Rule". The connection of a life in God and the vicissitudes of day-to-day living are vitally important. It is only through trust in the Lord that we may live exemplary lives and St Benedict shows us the way."

"But that is fraught with difficulty, Brother Ambrose. Living an exemplary life in God requires more than "The Rule", although, forsooth, it is a bedrock upon which we may grasp build lest we flounder in life's seas."

"Perhaps, you should dig deeper." Ambrose was warming to the discussion. "What is needed is a practical touchstone that guides you between the material and the sublime."

Thomas with head down bowed and eyes closed, thought about where these observations inevitably led, allowing the wisdom of the words to settle. The serene ambiance of the garden, complete with the melodious singing of birds, and the scent of blooming flowers, added a calm reflective tone to the weight of their discussion.

Drawing a deep breath, he ventured, "Given these reflections on St. Benedict's teachings, might we not transition seamlessly to Aristotle's philosophy?"

Brother Ambrose smiled gently, "Indeed, Thomas. The interplay of faith and reason, tradition, and exploration, forms the tapestry of our spiritual journey."

Thomas stood up, mulling over the thoughts that had taken shape during their conversation. "Your insights have been invaluable, Brother Ambrose. But dusk is drawing near, and Vespers will be soon. I will return to the college and reflect on our conversation. I'm truly grateful."

Brother Ambrose gave a nod of understanding, his eyes reflecting the wisdom of many such discussions. "Our conversations always enrich my spirit, Thomas. I eagerly anticipate your lecture."

Thomas – The Church

Thomas left his rooms in Balliol and walked towards The University Church of St. Mary. Towering in the heart of the city, St. Mary's stood as the grandest of Oxford's parish churches, its silhouette a commanding presence on the skyline. With its expansive aisles, vast nave, and other compartments, the church was well-suited for hosting large gatherings, making it an ideal location for significant lectures and academic disputations. Today's lecture was expected to fill the nave to capacity, perhaps, even more.

Approaching St. Mary's, Thomas's contemplation shifted to the magnificent pulpit from which he would deliver his lecture. Hewn from solid stone, it stood with a distinctive hexagonal form, topped by a wooden canopy. The addition of the canopy was not just functional— amplifying his voice for all to hear—but it also was richly adorned with intricate carvings, underscoring the deep respect for which the Church held the spoken word.

Entering the vast building through the west doors, he momentarily halted, lifting his gaze to the masterfully crafted rose window overhead. With measured steps, he traversed the nave, absorbing its solemnity. The crossing, where nave and transepts met, lay before him, leading him towards the chancel, the domain of the clergy and the choir.

Drawing nearer to the chancel, he passed through the rood screen's gated passage, a symbolic barrier between the laity and the sacred heart of the church. The chancel, with its high altar, choir, and the renowned pulpit, never failed to invoke reverence in Thomas. Though he had frequented St. Mary's, today, the majesty of the cathedral enveloped him with an intensity he hadn't previously experienced.

Pausing at the rood screen, the breathtaking east window captivated him. The Crucifixion, rendered in vivid stained glass, dominated the scene, flanked by smaller panes that immortalized the apostles in vibrant hues.

Somewhat overwhelmed by the sanctity of his chosen setting, he bowed slightly in reverence to the altar and proceeded to the pulpit, extracting lecture notes from his black gown's long sleeves. His attire, while formal, bore the modesty befitting his status: a master's student without the embellishments of a hood or cap.

The Pulpit in St. Mary's

Although his lecture was yet an hour away, he noticed individuals filtering into the church. Among them, he noted monks, clergy, and academicians from Balliol and its sister institutions within the University of Oxford. He noticed very few students but supposed that they would begin to arrive closer to the start of his lecture.

Thomas – The Lecture Begins

As he readied himself to begin the lecture, Thomas faced the altar and whispered a prayer, hoping his words would enlighten rather than divide. He was acutely aware of the complexity of his chosen topic; after all, theology, philosophy, and logic were intricate themes. He sought divine guidance, praying for the clarity, precision, and empathy to articulate these profound concepts.

As he meditated upon his lecture, he noted that the angle of the sun through the east window, and the huge crowd reducing to a trickle, indicated time for the lecture to begin. As he prepared mentally, the Vicar of St. Mary's joined him in the pulpit.

"Gentlemen and lady guests, I extend a warm welcome to you all at St. Mary's. Today, we are privileged to hear from an esteemed lecturer from Balliol College, Thomas of Hereford. His chosen subject for this year's Trinity Lecture is *The Confluence of Aristotelian Logic with Christian Theology: Pathways to Greater Understanding or Roads to Heresy?* After deep contemplation and prayer, Thomas presents this lecture. Let us heed his insights."

Thomas scanned the audience. To his surprise, near the front, sat his father, Sir Willem. But Sir Willem's stern look did not convey pride. "He is still doubting my path in academia," Thomas's mind whispered.

Next, his gaze settled on Brother Ambrose, his friend and mentor. Instead of the expected warmth, Ambrose looked unusually tense.

At the back, a group of students whispered amongst themselves. Their excitement was clear. They were ready to challenge.

Preparing himself to address the diverse assembly, Thomas began.

"Gentlemen, lady guests, students, and faculty, thank you for being here. My intent today is simple: to explore how Aristotelian Logic and Christian Theology intersect, and how, together, they can provide us a richer understanding of our faith."

He took a deep breath and continued, "St. Benedict once said, *'To listen and to act on God's word makes one wise.'* And also, *'God's wish is for us to be saved and to turn to him.'* Let's keep these words in mind as we journey through today's topic.

Aristotle believed in grounding religious discussions in worldly knowledge. He said, *'When discussing religion, it's good also to consider what the world around us tells us.'*

This means that when we read the Bible, Aristotle would encourage us to also consider the foundations from whence it came."

Thomas paused, letting his words sink in.

"Now, Aristotle also believed that everything has a potential and can reach its full form. In fact, he pondered on the nature of God, noting that while God is singular, He also embodies the Holy Trinity. It is like a dance between what we know from our faith and what philosophy teaches us."

Another brief pause.

"Aristotle saw God as the ultimate force, free from worldly constraints. This is similar to our understanding of God in Christianity. Even Aristotle's idea that our souls and bodies are linked fits well with Christian beliefs.

So, the question is not whether Aristotle's ideas clash with Christian teachings. The fact is that his logic adds depth to our faith."

Thomas – Reactions

Thomas paused, collecting his thoughts before presenting his final summary and conclusion.

"Since Aristotle's logic and his physics primarily address the observable world, they do not conflict with Christian doctrines concerning God or the afterlife. Therefore, positioning Aristotle's philosophy parallel with Christian thought is not far-fetched, as long as we emphasize those facets of his thinking that are consistent with the Church.

In essence, Aristotle provides us with a compass, guiding us through the convergence of his philosophy and logic with the theological tenets of Christianity, offering us a path to wisdom rather than division. Thank you."

The moment Thomas finished; reactions rippled through the congregation. While most showed their appreciation with enthusiastic applause, pockets of discord emerged. From the back of the nave, a cluster of students voiced their dissent. Their shouts, though restrained, perhaps out of reverence for the sanctity of the surroundings, still carried clear messages:

"Heretic!"

"Pretender!"

"Aristotle is not God!"

Some of the monks, too, joined the chorus of disapproval, declaring, "Blasphemy! We adhere to St. Benedict, not to your false prophet, Aristotle."

The agitated students swiftly rose from their seats, making a disorderly departure through the imposing western doors. As they exited, their murmurs of censure echoed through the nave.

Among the observers, Sir Willem's gaze fixed intently on the unfolding spectacle. A self-satisfied smile crept onto his face. To him, this tumultuous response was irrefutable evidence of Thomas's unsuitability for academic life. Sir Willem resolved then and there: Thomas would either be drawn back to his rightful place at home, or he might find the journey back... unexpectedly challenging.

Thomas mulled over the varied reactions to his lecture, his feelings a whirl of pride and concern. While the majority of attendees seemed appreciative, his father's disapproving demeanour weighed heavily on him. Sir Willem's face revealed a perverse satisfaction to the students' and monks' jeers.

Brother Ambrose's countenance too, puzzled Thomas. It

was not one of support but almost of disappointment, especially when contrasted against the vocal objections of his fellow monks. The heated objections from the student body, while not entirely unforeseen, had been more fervent than he had anticipated.

Gently gathering his notes, Thomas descended from the pulpit. Instead of the sweeping success he had hoped for, the lecture had garnered notable dissent, especially from the two individuals he held in the highest regard: his father and Brother Ambrose.

Thomas – Reflections

As night fell over Oxford, Thomas stepped out of St. Mary's, his mind consumed by the lecture's events. The peace of his rooms beckoned, but hunger and contemplation led him to the *White Hart* tavern.

"Perhaps a small meal and a pint to settle my thoughts," he mused, passing across the threshold.

The warmth of the tavern's large fireplace with its burning logs greeted him as he approached the bar. "A pint of ale, some bread, and cheese, please."

"We've also got a nice lamb pottage tonight. Would you fancy some?"

The rare offering of meat made Thomas's decision easy. "Yes, thank you. That sounds perfect."

Settling near the fire in a large, overstuffed chair, Thomas noticed Brother Ambrose seated at a corner table, his hood drawn low. Meeting Ambrose's gaze, Thomas walked over and sat down at the monk's table.

"You spoke with conviction today. But the eyes often speak more than the mouth, and yours held a shadow of doubt," Ambrose observed.

"It wasn't doubt in the content, but I fear I might've lost some listeners."

Ambrose smiled. "This town is filled with bright minds, but few possess your heart and passion. Whether they heed your words now or later, you have planted a seed."

The two ate while they exchanged thoughts and reflections. As they prepared to leave, Ambrose suggested, "Reflect on today, but also look ahead. Sometimes, the most profound lessons emerge from such challenges."

They parted ways outside, and Thomas walked back to Balliol. When he arrived at his chambers, he found a folded note slipped under his door. He picked it up and read:

Thomas, this is urgent. I cannot even write this in my own hand. There's looming danger. Meet me tomorrow night, after dark, outside the abbey walls. Do not fail. – Ambrose

The handwriting was unfamiliar, and the signature informal. But the urgency was clear. His thoughts were distracted by movement outside his window: a fleeting shadow, perhaps someone passing by or merely a trick of the night. He decided to be cautious and bolted the door. With the note's mystery and the lecture's events, Thomas faced a restless night.

CHAPTER 4: WHISPERS OF DESTINY

In which we are introduced to Sister Agnes, her life in the convent, her curiosity, and her assistant from outside the convent walls.

The unusual warmth of spring pressed heavily upon the walls of the infirmary, causing Sister Agnes to fidget with the edge of her veil, seeking some slight relief. The weight of her coif headdress and the long, black tunic she wore seemed to stifle every attempt she made at finding a cooling breeze. As she skimmed the list of potions and herbs on her worktable, she mused about past warm seasons and wondered how she managed them.

Lost in her thoughts, and somewhat drowsy from the heat, she didn't notice the Abbess's entrance until the Mother Superior's voice snapped her back to the present.

"Sister Agnes," the Abbess began, her tone commanding attention.

"Mother!" Sister Agnes responded, her posture straightening. "To what do I owe the honour of your visit?"

"It's your outings, Sister," the Abbess replied with a hint of sternness. "There's talk about your frequent absences from the abbey and your closeness to Lady Beatrix."

Drawing herself up slightly, Sister Agnes answered, "Mother, Lady Beatrix has been a true benefactor to our infirmary. As our infirmarist I must appreciate that and, from time to time, show my appreciation by visiting with Lady Beatrix. Our interactions are purely out of respect and gratitude. Over time, a bond of friendship has formed, but our relationship remains above reproach."

"While Lady Beatrix de Aylesbridge and her family have been undeniably generous, you must exercise more discretion. The whispers and murmurs are becoming harder to ignore."

Feeling the weight of the Abbess's gaze, Sister Agnes nodded. "I understand, Mother. I will ensure that our interactions are more… discrete."

"Good. Once you have completed your inventory, come to my chambers. We need to discuss our stock and what might be needed for the infirmary."

"Of course, Mother. I shan't be long."

Sister Agnes, likely in her early 40s, possessed a distinctive beauty, even if at times she seemed enigmatic. Her habit could not conceal the lively spark in her eyes or the warmth of her frequent smiles, which endeared her to her fellow sisters.

A long-standing member of the abbey, she committed to her vows at the tender age of eighteen. Her deep interest in healing arts attracted the attention of Lady Beatrix de Aylesbridge, whose family's generous patronage to the abbey enabled Sister Agnes to receive advanced learning, bridging the roles of herbalist, nurse, anatomist, and healer. Their shared passion for medicine fostered a deep bond between the two women, solidifying a friendship that went beyond their roles within the abbey walls.

Isabel de Beauchamp – The Novice

Isabel de Beauchamp, the young novice assisting in the infirmary, seemed perpetually lost in thought these days. On this particular morning, her expression was even more troubled than usual, and Sister Agnes took note.

"What weighs on your mind, Sister?"

"It's that dream again, Sister Agnes. Lady Rosamunde keeps appearing in it. It feels as though she wants to tell me something, but the message always escapes me before I awaken."

Lady Rosamunde, known as "The Fair Rosamunde," was once the mistress to King Henry II. Originally, she was interred in the Chapter House of the Abbey; however, the Bishop of Lincoln, Hugh of Lincoln, deeming the honour unfitting of her status, ordered her remains to be relocated outside the church building, to within the abbey grounds.

Isabel looked down, her fingers nervously playing with the hem of her habit. "In my dream, I see her, before she is moved outside of the building. She lies on a catafalque, surrounded by a sea of candles. Suddenly, she sits upright, pointing directly at me. Just as she seems about to speak, I'm jolted awake."

Sister Agnes listened thoughtfully to her novice.

"There are no ghosts, Sister. The dream is the product of your imagination. Is there something troubling your conscience?"

Isabel hesitated and looked down at the floor.

"No… nothing. It is just the dream that troubles me."

It was clear to Sister Agnes that Isabel was troubled beyond the simplicity of a frightening dream.

Sister Agnes gently touched Isabel's arm; her eyes full of concern.

"Isabel, perhaps you should speak to the Confessor. He will be here on the morrow for our monthly confessions. It might bring you some solace to share your burdens with him."

Isabel looked hesitant for a moment, her eyes darting away, then nodded slowly. "Yes, Sister Agnes. Perhaps that might help. I... I just wish to find some peace."

Sister Agnes squeezed her arm reassuringly. "Seeking guidance and absolution can often light our path, sister. Remember, you're not alone in your journey."

Isabel took a deep breath, nodding in appreciation, hoping that the Confessor might provide the clarity she so desperately sought.

Novice Isabel – The Confession

The morning dawned, with bright sunshine casting its glow over a pristine blue sky. The warmth of recent days lingered as Isabel approached the chamber reserved for confessions with a hesitant step. Inside, the room was sparsely furnished. A table stood at the room's end, graced by a crucifix and fresh-cut flowers from the abbey's garden. Icons of the Blessed Saviour and Mother Mary adorned opposite walls. A chair and a prie-dieu, set a good distance apart, faced each other, a screen between them. In the chair, the Confessor, a seasoned priest familiar to the nuns from many years of service, sat waiting behind the screen.

"Good morning, Sister. What burdens your heart today?"

Isabel knelt at the prie-dieu, her hands clasped tightly in anticipation. With a tremor in her voice, she began, "Bless me, Father, for I have sinned. It has been one month since my last confession. I have harboured ill feelings towards my fellow sisters, neglected my prayers on more than one occasion, been remiss in fulfilling my duties, and displayed a lack of reverence towards Sister Agnes, who guides me in my service."

The confessor's voice was gentle but firm. "These lapses are not to be taken lightly, my child. For your acts of penance, you shall recite three *Hail Marys* and three *Our Fathers*. Additionally, I urge you to meditate upon *Chapter 7* of *The Rule of St. Benedict*, which delves into the virtue of humility. Recall the words of St. Benedict: *Whoever exalts himself shall be humbled, and whoever humbles himself shall be exalted.*"

Swallowing hard, Isabel added, "Father, my perceived sullenness by others is, in truth, deep, often silent, introspection. I am burdened with a concern that I find difficult to share, and I do not know where to turn."

The confessor leaned slightly forward behind his screen, a gesture of attentiveness. "Perhaps I can help you. What weighs so heavily on your heart?"

"Night after night for several weeks, I have been haunted by a recurring dream of *The Fair Rosamunde*. In my dream, she lies upon her catafalque, illuminated by the soft glow of surrounding candles. As I watch, she abruptly sits upright and points directly at me. She seems poised to relay some crucial message, yet every time, I awaken just before she speaks."

The confessor, after a thoughtful pause, responded, "Dreams can often be reflections of our inner anxieties, fears, or unresolved feelings. The image of Lady Rosamunde could symbolize something you are wrestling with internally. Perhaps an unresolved issue, or a choice you're hesitant to make. Lady Rosamunde's life was fraught with complexities; maybe you identify with her in some way or see her as a symbol of a challenge you're facing."

He continued, "While you must remember that dreams are not prophecies, they can sometimes be a window into our innermost soul, revealing things we might otherwise overlook. It would be wise to spend some moments in quiet reflection or keeping a journal about these dreams. Writing them down might provide insights when you read back on them.

But always remember, on this earth, there is only one true spirit we acknowledge: The Holy Spirit of the Trinity. The souls of the departed ascend to a divine realm, facing judgment by our Heavenly Father. Earthly spirits or ghosts, as some claim, do not linger amongst us."

Looking at Isabel compassionately, he added, "Furthermore, engage in meditative prayer. In your meditations, visualize Lady Rosamunde's image and ask God to provide clarity about its meaning. In time, with patience and faith, understanding may come. And remember, my child, our Lord is always with you. Lean on Him and the community around you for support."

Concluding the confession, he pronounced, "In the name of The Father, The Son, and The Holy Spirit, go forth in peace and introspection. Amen."

Isabel – After the Confession

As Isabel walked slowly back to the infirmary, she pondered the Confessor's words. Though she had hoped for more concrete guidance, she understood the weight of interpretation and action rested upon her shoulders. Immersed in her thoughts and silent prayers, she yearned for clarity from her recurring dream. She hoped the next time the apparition of Rosamunde appeared; God might lead her to some resolution to her internal turmoil.

By the time she reached the infirmary, dusk had already settled. Sister Agnes awaited her arrival.

"Evening approaches, Sister," Sister Agnes remarked gently. "Let's attend Vespers, then join our sisters for supper."

The two walked at a measured pace, following the path that skirted the abbey walls. They entered the chapel for evening prayers, after which, they walked with the other nuns to the refectory, the communal dining hall where the sisters assembled for meals.

Once the meal was over, the Abbess recited Psalm 42:

As the deer pants for streams of water,

so my soul pants for you, my God.

My soul thirsts for God, for the living God.

When can I go and meet with God?

My tears have been my food

day and night,

while people say to me all day long,

'Where is your God?'

These things I remember,

as I pour out my soul:

how I used to go to the house of God

under the protection of the Mighty One

with shouts of joy and praise

among the festive throng.

Why, my soul, are you downcast?

Why so disturbed within me?

Put your hope in God,

for I will yet praise him,

my Saviour and my God.

Isabel found the Abbess' selection of the evening reading, for some reason she could not comprehend, particularly comforting. She was especially drawn to the end of the psalm,

Why, my soul, are you downcast?

Why so disturbed within me?

Put your hope in God,

for I will yet praise him,

my Saviour and my God.

Perhaps, she just felt weary from the emotional weight of the day. Isabel decided to retire early. Once nestled in her bed, sleep quickly claimed her. It was not long before the familiar dream returned. The setting unchanged, she anxiously awaited the moment Lady Rosamunde would rise.

She did rise and this time, Rosemunde spoke.

CHAPTER 5: VEIL OF NIGHT

It was after curfew when Thomas left his rooms at Balliol College, bound for Rewley Abbey. Tucked within the sleeve of his gown was the peculiar letter slipped under his door on the previous night. As he approached the Balliol Postern Gate, now sealed for the night, he barely noticed Old Cedric, the college's porter, standing guard. Lost in thought about Brother Ambrose's odd way of reaching out, Cedric's familiar voice snapped him back to reality.

"Good evening, Master Thomas. Out for a late stroll, are we?"

Startled, Thomas replied, "Yes, Cedric. I am heading to Rewley Abbey to see one of the monks."

"Be cautious, sir. These streets can be treacherous after dark."

"Thank you for the warning. I'll be on my guard." With a nod, Thomas continued, the mysterious note weighing on his mind.

Thomas – Death Awaits in the Shadows of the Abbey Walls

As Thomas neared the Abbey, still lost in the incessant thoughts in his mind, a sinister shadow crept in the deep shadows cast by the towering walls. Nudging at the gate with one hand, the door remained fixed, so he set the lantern on the ground and pushed with both hands. Just as the door gave way, a dark figure grabbed Thomas by the shoulders, shoving him to the ground and toppling the lantern. Having endured a unusually dry spring, the grass quickly caught the lantern's flame.

Caught off guard and now grappling with both the unexpected fire and the sudden appearance of his assailant, Thomas barely registered the sensation of cold steel piercing his chest. The subsequent blow he never felt. Collapsing to the ground, the blood throbbing freely from his wounds quenched the encroaching flames. As his vision faded, Thomas managed one last glimpse of his attacker's face before the cold embrace of death overtook him.

CHAPTER 6: DAWN OF DREAD

The report of the coroner's inquest, conducted by deputy coroner Adam de Wallingford into Thomas' murder was short and to the point:

Coroner's Roll 173.

It came to pass in the nighttime of Friday after the feast of St. George, in the 23rd year of the reign of King Edward, Thomas of Hereford died outside the walls of Rewley Abbey, within the parish bounds of St. Thomas the Martyr. On the following day, his body was inspected by Adam de Wallingford, the appointed coroner. The deceased bore two grievous wounds, each puncturing nearly through the core of his form.

A subsequent inquest was promptly convened on that same day before the aforementioned coroner, drawing jurors from our neighbouring parishes, namely St. Thomas the Martyr, St. Mary Magdalen, St. Michael at the North Gate, and St. Giles. The unanimous testimony of these jurors attests that the departed Thomas, on the past Friday, passed through the Balliol Postern, seemingly en route to Rewley Abbey. It was during this journey that some unknown assailant or assailants approached him, striking him with a long blade, piercing perilously close to his heart. Such grievous injuries led to his immediate demise on that Friday, yet it is of note that he had received all due ecclesiastical rites. The identity of the murderer or murderers remains shrouded in mystery, allowing their escape without trace. No belongings or evidence could be procured pertaining to these elusive individuals.

Undersheriff Alric the Bald examined the report. As he started to consider his investigation he walked to the coroner's rooms and asked to see the transcript of the inquest.

"I need more details, Master Adam. This is going to be very difficult case to solve. Thomas' gown, face, and hands were badly burned and the surrounding grass, dried by this damned heat burned rapidly, covering any traces that might aid   me."

"Of course, Undersheriff. Here is the full transcript for you to read for yourself."

Date: *23rd of April, the morrow of the feast of St. George, in the 23rd year of the reign of King Edward.*

Presiding: *Coroner Adam de Wallingford*

1. Introduction

Deputy Coroner Adam de Wallingford:

We convene today to scrutinize the circumstances surrounding the tragic demise of Thomas of Hereford, a lecturer at Balliol College. It is our lawful duty to understand the manner and cause of Master Thomas' death.

2. Examination of the Body:

Deputy Coroner Adam de Wallingford:

The scene I surveyed bore signs of a grass fire, likely instigated by the tipping of Master Thomas' lantern. His blood-soaked gown shielded him from the worst of the fire, yet his face and hands suffered significant burns. Two profound stab wounds were the definitive cause of his death, made by a long, possibly dagger-like, blade.

3. Testimony of Old Cedric, the Balliol Postern Porter:

Deputy Coroner Adam de Wallingford:

Kindly describe your role at Balliol College, Old Cedric.

Old Cedric:

I serve as the night porter, sir.

Deputy Coroner Adam de Wallingford:

Did you encounter the deceased on that fateful night?

Old Cedric:

Indeed. Master Thomas passed the Postern gate, seemingly deep in thought. He mentioned meeting a monk at Rewley Abbey, possibly Brother Ambrose, with whom he once admitted to having a disagreement.

Deputy Coroner Adam de Wallingford:

Thank you, Cedric. You are dismissed.

4. Witness Testimony: Near Rewley Abbey

Deputy Coroner Adam de Wallingford:

Anyone present during the incident near Rewley Abbey?

John of Witney:

I can recount my experience, sir.

Deputy Coroner Adam de Wallingford:

Please proceed, John.

John of Witney, shepherd:

I noticed an odd glow by the Abbey walls and perceived sounds indicative of a confrontation. However, my duty to my restless flock prevented me from investigating.

Deputy Coroner Adam de Wallingford:

Thank you, John. Any others?

Gilbert the Bladesmith:

I heard a commotion near the Abbey wall. Having

finished sharpening the abbey's knives, I was departing and did not think much of the noise.

Deputy Coroner Adam de Wallingford:

Thank you, Gilbert.

5. Account of the Scene Discovery:

Deputy Coroner Adam de Wallingford:

Brother Ambrose, please come forward.

Brother Ambrose:

I found Master Thomas near the Abbey. His grievous state was evident, with burn injuries and signs of a violent stabbing.

Deputy Coroner Adam de Wallingford:

Thank you, Brother Ambrose.

6. Deliberation of the Jurors:

Deputy Coroner Adam de Wallingford:

In light of the presented evidence and accounts, I request the jurors deliberate and provide a verdict. A possible conclusion is a verdict of homicide due to violent knife wounds by an unidentified assailant.

7. Conclusion:

The tragic loss of Thomas, a revered scholar, poses questions. Was it Brother Ambrose, with whom there was known discord? The bladesmith Gilbert, skilled in the use of blades? A disgruntled student, or even family? We await the jury's conclusion.

Spokesman for the Jury:

We believe that Thomas met his end through violent means. Our verdict: homicide, resulting from brutal stab wounds delivered by a person or persons presently unknown.

Deputy Coroner Adam de Wallingford:

Thank you. Master Scribe, prepare the transcript for my approval and ensure that it's archived. This inquest is concluded.

End of Transcript

And so, with the conclusion of the inquest, the body of Thomas of Hereford was prepared for burial and conveyed, after one secret stop, to St. Mary's church for the funeral mass.

The Undersheriff - Reactions

The undersheriff, still puzzled over the lack of evidence beyond an evident murder, "by person or persons unknown" considered his next move. He decided that he would attend the funeral and burial with the hope that someone attending one or both might somehow give himself away as the killer.

In that hope, he was, of course, disappointed.

The next day undersheriff Alric began his routine investigation. His first stop was the *White Hart*. As he entered the tavern, he noted a group of students off in a corner of the room heatedly discussing the events of the previous two days.

"You know that sheriff will come after us," one student prompted.

"Of course, but he'll find nowt at the college."

"Surely, he knows how we greeted Master Thomas. That will make him suspicious."

"So, let him be as suspicious as he likes. There is nothing to find but talk."

The undersheriff walked to the bar. "A pint of ale, please."

The barmaid pulled the pint and brought it to the undersheriff. "Here. Have you heard the talk going around about the murder, then?"

"I have heard a lot of talk, but it's all fancy and imagination. Nobody knows what really happened and the coroner's inquest shed little light."

Taking his ale, he walked over to a large, comfortable chair by the fire, thinking about what he knew and what questions still remained unanswered. *For that matter, what unthought-of questions still remained unasked?*

From the other side of the room, two men from the town were conversing in barely restrained whispers.

"It's obvious who, or, rather, what killed the lecturer."

"And what might that be, I ask ye?"

"Remember when the sheriff hanged John the Highwayman last month?"

"Aye. It could have been him comin' back a-seekin' vengeance."

"But why, the lecturer? He had nothing to do with the catchin' and hangin'."

"It's a warnin' to all of us. There will be more dead before long, and that's a fact."

"Those wounds weren't from no knife. They was from the claws of a demon!"

"And the fire! Do not forget the fire! John's spirit is among us, shaped like a demon from Hell. Mark me, Geordie, there'll be more slashins and burnins afore this month is out."

The sheriff had heard enough. "These superstitious town-folk always conjure demons, spirits, or a cursed knife as the cause of a murder," he mused, "but they don't know the facts any more than I do."

He finished his pint and started out the door.

"Sheriff Alric! Find yer killer yet?"

"Now what are you expectin' Maxwell? It's been but three days, and we have naught for clues."

"I'll give you a clue. Look no farther than that abbey. Those monks in there… always doin' mysterious things. Human sacrifice, mayhap. I don't know and I don't want to, but mind ye, Thomas was killed right by their high wall. And don't forget the fire and how it burned poor Thomas. Fire called up by those monks and their infernal rites, it was."

The undersheriff nodded sadly. These rumours were growing, both in number and in wild, improbable guesses. Trouble was, he was not doing much better.

CHAPTER 7: A DIVINE INQUIRY

In which we hear Sister Agnes's decision to investigate the murder and meet her unlikely assistant.

Sister Agnes stood in the convent chapel; her prayers were interrupted by a summons from the abbess.

"Thank you for coming, Sister Agnes."

"Of course, Mother. How can I assist you?"

"I have troubling news. There has been a murder."

"Sadly, murders in Oxford town are not a rarity. Why does this particular one concern the abbey?"

"The victim was a Balliol lecturer. But what is most concerning is the location of the crime."

"Where did it happen?"

"Outside Rewley Abbey. Rumours are circulating that one of our own brothers might be involved."

"That is preposterous. Why would any of our devout brothers commit such an act?"

"I agree, it is improbable. But rumours have a way of spreading, and this one is becoming troubling."

"When did this occur?"

"Three days ago. The matter has been kept discreet thus far."

"And why bring this to my attention, Mother?"

"Discretion is crucial, Agnes. The deceased's family has requested that you examine the body before burial."

"I'm unsure of what insights I might offer them."

"It is not a matter of insights, but of respect. The high-born family has been generous to our abbey. Their request should be honoured."

"A noble family? Who is the deceased?"

"Thomas of Hereford. Given our ties and your reputation as a healer, their request is understandable. It is known that you're skilled with remedies, herbs, and treatments. Your talents are unmatched in Oxfordshire. It is no wonder they seek your perspective. Especially considering his father is Sir Willem."

"I understand the gravity, Mother. I will inform my novice to make preparations. When should we expect the body?"

"He's already here, and your novice is tending to him. But first, take a moment in the chapel to seek guidance and wisdom for this difficult task ahead."

Sister Agnes – The Autopsy

After seeking guidance in the chapel, Agnes returned to the infirmary. Thomas lay upon her worktable, completely shrouded by a cloth. Beside him, the young novice, Isabel, stood with her eyes firmly shut, her face pale.

"Isabel," Agnes began gently, "we must remember that our bodies are merely temples, destined to crumble and return to dust. While Thomas' body remains here, his soul has ascended to Heaven. Now, it is our task to understand how his earthly vessel met its end."

Isabel replied hesitantly, "This is all new and unsettling for me, Sister."

Agnes's tone held a hint of sternness. "Our duty to the family and to God compels us to find out how Thomas died. Cut the cloth away from the wound, Isabel. We will examine it without further disturbance to his form. Then, fetch your quill and a piece of parchment. Write down what I tell you and ensure that your Latin is precise."

Isabel took a sharp knife from the small table situated near Thomas' head and, under Sister Agnes' guidance, made an incision in the cloth to reveal the area around the wounds. Beneath the cloth, the two grievous marks on Thomas's chest were painfully evident.

The hot, dry weather combined with scents in the room–the sharp tang of vinegar from cleaning the worktable, the smoky aroma of incense burned for purification and blessing, and the herbal fragrances applied to Thomas' body–felt overpowering. They caused Isabel's head to swim slightly and her eyes to water. Nevertheless, she steeled herself, moving to the writing table situated close on to the head of the main worktable, preparing her quill, ink, and parchment to write down Sister Agnes' observations.

The infirmary was spacious. Its scrubbed, whitewashed walls hosted two large windows that allowed the sun to spill in, blanketing the room with a warm, golden hue. The room's focal point was the substantial table upon which Thomas rested. While beneath one window, another table stood laden with tools and materials Agnes employed in preparing medicinal herbs and potions. Another wall was adorned with shelves filled with packaged remedies, and another section, close to the primary table's head, contained tools vital to Agnes' healing craft.

After offering a prayer for the soul of Thomas and wisdom to understand what she may discover, Agnes used an instrument resembling a long, hollow probe, to examine the depths of the two wounds delicately. As she gently probed the two wounds she dictated to Isabel.

"The upper wound was inflicted first. It is deeper, perhaps indicative of a surge of anger or intent. The one below is shallower. The first strike alone might have been enough to be lethal. There are signs that the blade was twisted upon extraction from the second wound; the tissue surrounding this wound is more disturbed than the other." Isabel diligently noted down Agnes' observations.

Using a pair of forceps, Agnes carefully probed the shallower wound. "There's something here... lodged against the rib." She meticulously extracted a small shard.

"This appears to be a fragment of a knife blade. Judging by its size and shape, the blade was likely slender and keen-edged. The tip might have been honed to such a fine point that it became fragile, more susceptible to breakage. This fragment seems to be made of silver. It suggests that Thomas met his end with what might be a ceremonial dagger; perhaps something akin to a rondel dagger crafted for ceremonial purposes?" She wrapped the shard in a small piece of cloth and placed it on the shelf with her healing tools.

"We've gleaned important insights, Sister Isabel. Thomas met a brutal end, driven by rage and anger. The initial, likely fatal blow was delivered with full force, but by the second strike, the killer's fury was waning, though not entirely spent. That strike likely was interrupted by a rib, and the killer had to twist the blade in order to extract it causing the blade to fracture.

Once his victim lay lifeless, and the grass alight, the murderer made his exit. The saturated state of the garments implies a heart wound. The heart would have persisted in pumping blood until his final moments, saturating the fabric and hindering the fire from fully claiming Thomas. The knife was not found in or near the body so the killer must have taken it with him to dispose of later."

As Agnes concluded, Lady Beatrix stepped into the workroom.

"Mother Superior mentioned you might be here. Sir Willam asked me to check on your progress. What have you discovered?"

"We've uncovered a significant amount, my lady. Now we understand the manner in which his son was killed and can even infer the killer's state of mind. This information will undoubtedly aid the undersheriff and proctor in their pursuit of justice. It seems the fire was an unintended impediment for the assailant. I believe he had hoped it would erase all evidence of the crime. But he had not anticipated the blood, spewing from Thomas' injured heart, drenching his robes, and thus preserving vital evidence."

Agnes gently pulled back a section of the cloth veiling Thomas's chest. Isabel visibly recoiled, diverting her gaze. Beatrix, however, stepped closer for a better view.

Agnes remarked with evident satisfaction, "Observe, my lady. There are no external bruises or marks on Thomas, save for the knife wounds. This suggests a swift assault, from ambush, rendering Thomas defenceless. We are looking for someone, familiar with violence, with a deep hatred of Thomas."

She refrained from mentioning the shard of blade or the whispers implicating a monk from Rewley Abbey. However, Beatrix, with her finger ever on the pulse of town gossip, responded to Agnes' comments.

"You're no doubt aware, Sister, of the speculations circulating through the town? Some suggest that one of the monks from the abbey might be responsible for Thomas's demise. The porter at the gate Thomas passed through even mentioned some quarrel with a brother."

"Yes, my lady," Agnes responded, "I was privy to such

murmurs. At first, I gave them little heed. But after examining Thomas, I find the notion of such a vicious act from one of the compassionate brothers at Rewley to be highly improbable."

Beatrix seemed lost in thought for a moment, then: "With everything we've uncovered, Sister, can Sir Willam now lay his son to rest?"

"Yes, Lady Beatrix. I will inform Mother so she can contact Sir Willam and his family. Isabel, once you have finalized your notes– and don't overlook the discovery made by Lady Beatrix and me– jot down my conclusions and leave them for me. I will present them to Mother Superior."

Isabel looked as relieved as she felt, "As you wish, Sister." She departed the workroom with evident relief. The weight of death in the chamber was stifling.

The autopsy's completion left Sister Agnes with some small sense of closure. However, there still were questions clawing at her thoughts. *Why, for example, did the killer wish to meet at Rewley Abbey? And who could build such a hatred for an insignificant lecturer that it resulted in what must have been a blinding rage and desperate violent attack?*

Most important, though, where was the knife that left a small shard of its tip in the rib of Thomas? That certainly cleared any monk of the murder. No monk could afford such a silver ceremonial dagger. *But, if not, who could?*

She quickly put such questions out of her mind. The autopsy was over, and she had more important tasks in service to her God and to the living. Agnes silently appreciated Lady Beatrix's presence. Despite her noble lineage, the lady displayed a commendable resilience in the face of grim tasks.

The Knife –Hidden, Found and Hidden Again

As Thomas' killer fled from Rewley Abbey, his primary thought was disposing of the dagger that he had used to kill Thomas. Having stolen the dagger from a knight so well-known and near him, he knew that he must avoid being caught with it at all costs.

As he ran, he found himself near the stream that flowed under the old stone bridge near the Aylesbridge lands. As he approached the bridge and looked down into the water flowing beneath it, he took the dagger and flung it as hard as he could into the stream and away from the bridge. Not hesitating, the murderer ran at top speed across the bridge and into the town.

Young Edmund, whose mother laboured in the kitchen of the household of Lady Beatrix de Aylesbridge, was going fishing.

His head swimming with visions of knights and adventure, and the bright sunshine bathing the manor house grounds in a bright pale-yellow glow, young Edmund ran across the well-manicured lawns and made for the lake on the grounds which he knew to be well-stocked with fat fish, ripe for the catching.

But such was not his final destination. Indeed, the lake was not wholly contained on Aylesbridge lands. It was fed by a stream and that was where Edmund was heading. He passed from the lawns of the manor house and still running, he progressed under the canopy of ancient trees that lined the trail to the stream.

There, in his secret fishing spot, he hoped to catch a very big fish that his mother would prepare for supper. But the fish he caught would not be eaten that night or any other but would end up in Edmund's trunk with his clothes and other treasures.

The boy threw his line several times without success. The fish, it seemed, were not biting today. Then his line snagged on something, clearly not a fish, but rather something lodged in the muck and stones at the bottom of the stream bed.

He wiggled his pole until the object broke loose. He brought it to the surface of the stream, astonished at what he saw. It was a jewelled silver dagger with its tip broken off. And now, it was all his. *Was he being told by some mysterious force that he was, indeed, destined for knighthood? Or, perhaps, something more?*

Picking up his fishing pole and the knife, Edmund ran back toward the cottage he shared with his mother on the edge of the manor house grounds. As he approached the cosy stone cottage, he slowed down, being careful to watch out for his mother. His mother, Margaret, was the head poulterer for the manor, caring for the fowl that frequently graced the noble table. The cottage was very close to the poultry pens.

He walked slowly up the flower-lined path to the cottage. As he approached, he heard his mother clucking to the fowls. It must be feeding time, and that meant that his mother was in the pens behind the house. Edmund slipped quietly in through the front door and tiptoed across the living room with its big cheerful fireplace. Wood was laid in the fireplace but there was no fire, and, with this weather, there would not be until autumn took over from what promised to be a long hot, dry summer.

On the other side of the room, just past the small kitchen, he silently opened his bedroom door and went in.

At the foot of Edmund's bed sat a sea chest, its time-worn wood bearing the marks of countless ocean voyages. It had once belonged to his father, a seaman lost to the waves long ago. The chest, both an emotional reminder of his father and a connection to the adventurous tales of the sea, now contained Edmund's clothes and treasures.

He went to the small table sitting next to his bed. A sturdy wooden bedframe supported a mattress filled with straw. Under the table, from a secret shelf that Edmund had made himself, he took the hidden key and used it to open the chest. He picked up the pieces of clothing, placed the dagger on the floor of the chest, and carefully replaced the neatly folded clothes on top. After re-locking the old sea chest, Edmund returned the key to its hiding place and went back to the fowl pens to greet his mother.

Margaret, fondly known as Maggie among friends, was wrapping up her morning routine with the poultry. She went inside the cottage and collected a stack of Edmund's clean clothes. As a senior staff member at the manor, she was privileged to have decent attire for her son and herself.

Not that the clothes were new… in fact, some were a bit time worn, but Maggie knew how to keep a house and how to get the most from hand-me-down clothes. All it takes, she mused, was a needle and thread and a bit of extra care. Extra care was Maggie's forte. She exercised it in all she did, from her duties at the manor house to the keeping of her own hearth and home.

She fetched the key from its hiding place and opened the old sea chest. As she removed the clothes in the chest to reorganize them with the freshly folded ones, she dwelt briefly on her husband lost these many years to the sea. Her reverie was broken abruptly as she saw the jewel-encrusted dagger at the bottom of the chest.

Dropping the folded clothes on the bed, she called out to Edmund, "Edmund, lad, where are ye?"

"In the kitchen, mother."

She held up the dagger. "And what's this, then?"

"It is mine, Mother! I found it in the stream. It must have belonged to a knight from long ago."

Maggie's voice held a hint of her origins in the Scottish Lowlands when she replied, "Knight, ye say? It's nay so auld as ye might think!" Her brogue became even more pronounced as she continued, "This is nay a toy for you to play with. Where did you truly find this?"

"In the creek, where I fish mother," Edmund protested. "Look how it shines! Give it back!"

Sternly, "I will not. I'll be takin' it to the lady of the manor. She'll know what to do." And with that, she marched off with the dagger toward the manor house.

Maggie and Beatrix – In the Garden

Margaret entered the manor house kitchen. The room was vast and arranged with meticulous care. Opposing stone hearths, each encompassing an entire wall, stood ready to receive large copper pots with various foods for cooking, their dancing flames casting a warm glow and filling the room with the aroma of burning wood. The kitchen was very warm, and Maggie found herself quite uncomfortable.

Spanning the centre of the room were two sizeable oak worktables, worn smooth from years of use, upon which ingredients were prepared and dishes assembled.

Arrayed methodically around the room were smaller trestle tables, dedicated to specific tasks, such as chopping or grinding spices. Nearby stood hefty wooden basins, often replenished with fresh water from the well, serving as the primary source of water for cleaning and preparation of the food.

Copper pots and pans hung from hooks on the walls, catching and reflecting the firelight, while shelves lined with earthenware jars held an array of dried herbs and spices. This kitchen, bustling with activity from dawn till dusk, was the unseen heart of the manor.

Maggie looked around for someone to take her message to Lady Beatrix. She spied one of the footmen, an older man named Samuel.

"Samuel, I must get a message to Lady Beatrix. It is really quite urgent. Can you help me?"

"Of course, Maggie. In fact, I was just on my way up. I have been summoned to attend the front door. How may I help you?"

"Edmund found this dagger in the stream near the bridge. Perhaps her ladyship can help decide what to do with it. The blade appears to be of silver, and there are jewels all over the handle. And look… the tip is broken off."

"I will get this to my lady at once. Perhaps you should stay here for a moment and await her answer." Samuel marched toward the back stairs and disappeared up the dark passageway.

Moments later he returned without the dagger. "My lady insists that you meet her in the garden at once, but you must tell nobody."

"Thank you, Samuel," and Maggie was away.

The garden behind the manor was a symphony of colours and scents, with neatly arranged beds of fragrant herbs, vibrant blossoms, and tall, whispering trees providing welcome cool shade. Stone pathways meandered between the flower beds, leading to secluded nooks where one could sit and contemplate the beauty of the place. It was in one of these shaded alcoves, on a stone bench surrounded by blooming roses, that Lady Beatrix chose to meet Maggie. Samuel, Beatrix's footman, stood off to the side, out of earshot.

Maggie rose to meet her mistress.

"Maggie, how came you by this dagger?" There was a clear sense of urgency in the question.

"Edmund found it in the stream by the bridge, my lady. He brought it home and secreted it in his chest. I discovered it when tending to his clothes."

"This must remain between us, Maggie. I suspect it to be of great significance, and there is someone to whom I must show it directly."

"As you wish, my lady. I have no desire for it, and certainly not for Edmund to have it."

"Your diligence in bringing this to my attention might have far-reaching implications. Therefore, I wish to acknowledge your service. You shall train your assistant to assume the role of poulterer. With the recent departure of our kitchen mistress, I see no one better than you to fill her post. Your literacy skills and unwavering service have not gone unnoticed. Make arrangements to inhabit the kitchen mistress' dwelling and have your assistant relocate to your current abode. I will send word of the changes to the kitchen."

With a tear in her eye and her Scottish brogue momentarily absent, "Your generosity is boundless, my lady. You shan't regret your decision."

"I have no doubt, Maggie. Now, I must away. Samuel! Tell the groom that I will require my carriage at once." And as quickly as she had appeared, Lady Beatrix was gone.

Sister Agnes – Decision

Sister Agnes sat in the chapel, her thoughts wandering over recent events—chiefly the request for her to conduct an autopsy on the body of Thomas of Hereford. The weight of her thoughts drove her to seek solace in the peaceful quiet of the chapel. Engrossed in her meditation, she barely noticed when her novice, Isabel, slipped in.

Sensing someone else's presence, Agnes glanced up. "How may I assist you, my child?"

"Sister, Lady Beatrix awaits you in the infirmary," Isabel whispered. "She insisted it was urgent, otherwise I would not have interrupted your reflections."

"I understand, Isabel. Assure her that I will be with her anon." With a nod, Isabel left as silently as she came. After a few moments of gathering her thoughts, Sister Agnes rose, walking slowly and contemplatively to the infirmary to meet Lady Beatrix.

"Good day to you, my lady. To what do I owe this surprise visit? Does something trouble you?"

"Yes, sister. Something troubles me very much." She walked over to a worktable, Sister Agnes close behind. "Look at this dagger. The child of one of the servants found it in the stream by the old stone bridge while he was fishing. He brought it home and his mother discovered it and brought it to me. After examining it carefully, I concluded that it could be particularly important evidence in the death of Thomas."

Sister Agnes picked up the dagger and examined it minutely. Then she fetched a small, clear piece of polished glass, its surface curved to a slight dome. It was a magnifying stone, a tool typically used by scholars and others to aid in examining small items such as texts or tiny stones.

In this instance, she believed it might provide a clearer view of the dagger's details. Holding the glass just above the dagger, she peered through it. The intricate designs and possible imperfections on the blade became significantly magnified, revealing features she might otherwise have overlooked.

"Whence did you procure that stone, Sister?"

"There are instances when I'm unable to cultivate specific herbs or prepare certain rare potions. In such times, I consult Elias of Warwick, the apothecary. He uses a stone similar to this to examine plants and herbs closely. Because of his advancing age, he also finds it helpful for reading minuscule texts. He gave it to me. I believe it might reveal much about the story of this dagger."

"But look you, Sister, the blade's tip is missing."

"Indeed, Lady Beatrix. I hold the missing piece. I extracted it from Thomas' body. Let us determine if it aligns with the remnant of the dagger you have brought."

Agnes delicately retrieved the shard, which rested atop a cloth on her workroom shelf. Positioning the blade onto the cloth, she used the magnifying stone and a pair of forceps meticulously to align the shard to the broken tip of the dagger. As the two fragments came closer, they seamlessly merged, revealing their perfect fit.

With charged intensity, Agnes declared, "Lady Beatrix, you have unquestionably discovered the instrument of murder. Let us now delve into its origins."

Agnes examined the blade using the magnifying stone, noting the minute scratches that marred the otherwise polished surface. They were not random; they followed a specific pattern, the kind that would come from being repeatedly sheathed and unsheathed from its scabbard.

Drawing from her knowledge of ceremonial daggers, she began to paint a mental picture.

"These scratches, they hint at a scabbard of dual nature," she murmured, mostly to herself. "The exterior, undoubtedly is adorned with silver and possibly other precious materials, fitting for a dagger of this stature."

"But the interior," she paused, squinting as she traced the lines on the blade with the tip of her finger, "It suggests a tougher, more durable lining. Likely a harder metal hidden beneath the beauty, responsible for these marks over time."

It was evident from her deduction that Agnes was not only familiar with the tools and symbols of rituals but also possessed an uncanny ability to read the stories they held.

"But Sister... who could possibly possess such a dagger?"

"Only a select few around here could afford or be given such a blade, my lady. I need time to reflect. We may be embarking on a perilous journey to uncover Thomas' killer. Seeking the truth may not be welcomed by those in power. I must seek divine guidance."

"I understand, Sister. Inform me once you have reached your conclusion," Lady Beatrix replied, her voice heavy with the weight of the matter, as she departed from the workroom.

In the sacred silence of the chapel, beneath the benevolent gaze of the Virgin Mary, it took Sister Agnes less than an hour to discover her path. A profound conviction welled up within her, whispering that the pursuit of truth was her sacred duty, no matter the dangers it entailed.

She returned to her workroom to find novice Isabel engrossed in the herb inventories.

"Isabel," Agnes began with a sense of urgency, "send word to Lady Beatrix. I am committed to unveiling the truth. Her counsel would be invaluable."

"Sister, there is no need. Lady Beatrix is in the garden. She told me that she would await your decision and welcomes your presence when you are ready."

Before Isabel could add another word, Sister Agnes was already on her way.

CHAPTER 8: HALLOWED HALLS, SILENT SECRETS

In which we follow Sister Agnes's initial inquiry within the scholastic community.

Lady Beatrix sat on a stone bench, ensconced within a sanctuary of shade trees amidst the blooming flora of the abbey garden. The sun's rays softened, lending a gentle glow to the surroundings.

Approaching her, Agnes began, "My lady, I thank you for your patience. My reflections in the chapel have only deepened my resolve to uncover what may be behind this grievous wrong. Your involvement would contribute much. Your stature and connections grant you access to places where my presence might stir undue whispers and speculations. I doubt such talk would be appreciated by Mother Superior."

Lady Beatrix met her gaze, determination evident in her eyes. "I am wholly committed, Sister. There are indeed realms open to me where your appearance might cause hesitancy. As well, the sisters of this abbey often engender reverence, which can sometimes inhibit candid conversations."

"I thank you my lady. I believe that we must begin by examining the atmosphere at Balliol. After all, Thomas was a lecturer there and there may be whispers that can guide our deliberations."

"I agree, sister. I know Hugh de Warkenby the Master of Balliol. My family has contributed to the college. I will visit Master Hugh on the pretext of endowing Thomas' replacement lecturer and see what I may learn."

Lady Beatrix – Master Hugh

The day was pleasantly cool and slightly overcast. Lady Beatrix's journey from Aylesbridge Hall to Balliol College was particularly pleasant. The hall itself was situated to the north of Oxford, nestled amidst the green fields and woodlands of the Cotswolds. As her carriage wheels moved along the dirt track, taking her through the Cotswolds' landscape of rolling hills and verdant pastures, Beatrix reflected on her family's legacy.

Although Balliol was in its emerging stages in the tapestry of Oxford's history, it was rapidly gaining renown, in part due to the generous patronage of families like the Aylesbridges. Her ancestors had long recognized the importance of education. Before their association with Balliol, they had extended their support to various studia, especially those dedicated to religious studies.

It was a useful mark of foresight, especially for her upcoming meeting with Master Hugh, Beatrix thought, for her family to have been interwoven with the growth of learning in the surrounding area.

The carriage moved from the tranquil countryside into the livelier streets of Oxford. The city was an expanding hub of academia, and she felt a swell of pride thinking of how her family had played a part in that.

Refocusing her attention on the task at hand, she considered how to approach Master Hugh, fortified by the weight of her family's legacy and the endeavour on which she was embarking. She must go smoothly from discussion of an endowment to picking up on any talk at the college regarding Thomas' death.

As Lady Beatrix approached, she saw Balliol College's

entrance: a simple archway set within a low stone wall, which delineated the boundary of the college. Above the arch, the college's newly adopted coat of arms. It combined the symbols of the Balliol family with those of the House of Bruce, a testament to the union of John de Balliol and his wife Dervorguilla, whose legacy now shaped the lives of young scholars within these walls.

Beyond the entrance, the college grounds were a mix of newer stone buildings and older timber-framed halls, showing its origins as a patchwork of smaller studia. Gravel pathways criss-crossed the green courtyard, leading to various quarters: the lecture halls, the modest chapel, and a few ancillary structures. Trees and shrubs had been planted here and there, creating a serene learning environment for its scholars.

Students, dressed in their academic gowns, hurried between buildings, some deep in conversation, others with noses buried in scrolls or manuscripts. The air was filled with a sense of scholarly pursuit and a touch of ambition. The college was in the early stages of building its identity.

Standing at the gateway, the college's porter, a tall man in a simple tunic, held his staff of office. Recognizing the coat of arms on the carriage, he nodded.

"Good day, Lady Beatrix," he greeted, bowing respectfully. "Master Hugh anticipates your visit. Please, allow me to escort you."

After disembarking with the porter's assistance, Beatrix turned to her groom. "Stay and await my return. I will return to the Hall once I conclude here."

"As you wish, my lady." Beatrix followed the porter into the college grounds.

The serenity of the gardens and their overall calming effect did not escape Beatrix's notice. They walked to a corner of the grounds where a newer, stone building housed chambers for the esteemed masters and doctors of the college. Near the end of the entry hall were Master Hugh's quarters.

His chambers, more spacious than most others in the building, had an antechamber furnished with unexpectedly comfortable chairs. Portraits adorned the walls: King Edward, Pope Boniface, and the college's founder, John de Balliol. A fireplace, ready for colder days ahead, was present, but the room retained a certain austerity.

Master Hugh entered through an arched doorway beneath the portrait of John, greeting Beatrix with a courteous bow. "My lady, our visits, though infrequent, are always a delight. How may I assist you?"

Master Hugh, in his academic gown, exuded an aura of stern distinction. He commanded respect, often appearing composed regardless of the situation. However, today, a hint of curiosity was evident in his eyes. This unexpected visit intrigued him.

"Master Hugh, it's always a pleasure. However, today it might be I who can assist you," Beatrix replied with a hint of mystery.

"Most intriguing. Let's discuss this in my study."

Upon entering, Beatrix noted the confined but bustling space, overflowing with books, scrolls, and parchments. The cluttered worktable, scattered with quills and ink pots, clearly demonstrated Master Hugh's heavy workload. Determined to make efficient use of their time, Beatrix braced herself to delve deeper, seeking any crucial insights Master Hugh might possess regarding the murder.

"Please be seated, my lady, and tell me of this assistance you speak of."

Beatrix calculated. She wanted to steer the conversation towards whatever she might learn of Thomas' death. After a brief survey of the room and a pause to gather her thoughts, she finally addressed the Master.

"Master Hugh, I'm here to discuss the tragic demise of one of your lecturers, Thomas of Hereford. It is a sorrowful loss. I've spoken with Sir Willam, and the depth of his grief over his son's passing is profound."

"Indeed, my lady. However, it is common knowledge that Sir Willam had serious reservations about his son's teaching pursuits."

"That may be, Master, but a father's love surpasses disagreements in vocation. Sir Willam mourns deeply. And it is in light of this tragedy that I bring forth an offer: My family wishes to endow a replacement for Thomas for as long as that individual serves Balliol."

Master Hugh was taken aback. Never in his wildest dreams had he envisioned such a silver lining to this grievous event. "My lady, I am momentarily at a loss for words. Are there any conditions your family wishes to impose with this generous act?"

"Only one condition, Master: that the beneficiary remains at Balliol as a devoted educator, mirroring the path Thomas had chosen or had perhaps already begun. Should he depart, the endowment will be withdrawn."

"Such a straightforward condition is quite acceptable, my lady. We will commence the search for a worthy successor to Thomas posthaste. But mark you, it will not be an easy task. Thomas was uniquely qualified for his position. Finding an apt replacement will be challenging."

"I trust your judgment and capabilities, Master. I am

confident you will navigate this adeptly. But now, let us consider more sombre matters. I seek to understand the young man whose successor I have chosen to endow. What insights can you offer about this bright flame, so abruptly extinguished?"

"Well, young Thomas was an introspective scholar, often absorbed in deep thought, yet he displayed moments of assertiveness. Perhaps you've heard of the varied reactions to his recent Trinity Lecture?"

"Yes, Master, I was present for the lecture. While I found it intellectually invigorating, I was taken aback by some responses, notably from the students." She paused, silently prompting Master Hugh to elucidate why the students displayed such vehement opposition to a lecture that, to her, seemed well-reasoned. The monks' reactions puzzled her further, but that was a matter for another time and place.

"Lady Beatrix, the truth is, there's profound resentment brewing among certain radical students."

"And what could be the root of this discontent, Master?"

"Thomas was swiftly ascending the academic ladder here at Balliol. Despite not completing his master's studies, he was already imparting knowledge to bachelor's students. These students perceived him as a peer, yet he had outpaced them at an astonishing rate. There's resentment stemming from being tutored—and having their scholastic futures shaped—by someone they deem as still, metaphorically speaking, 'wet behind the ears'."

"Hmmm," Beatrix mused, her expression thoughtful. "Would these more radical students have gone to the extent of committing murder to remove Thomas from their path?"

"It is hard to say, my lady. Students, particularly those

with extremist views, can be unpredictable in their actions. While I have not heard any concrete suspicions, it's an unfortunate reality that murder isn't a rarity in Oxford. Painfully, students often are embroiled in such incidents."

"If you come across any valuable information, Master, please relay it to me. It might provide some peace to Sir Willam."

Beatrix gave a slight bow to Master Hugh. "I appreciate your insights. Should you uncover any relevant details, I trust you will share them with me."

"Of course, my lady. I pledge to keep you informed. And I must express my heartfelt gratitude for your family's magnanimity."

Escorted by the porter, Beatrix headed for Balliol's entrance. She boarded her carriage and departed for the manor house.

Left in the courtyard, Master Hugh contemplated the true motive behind her visit. A mere letter would have sufficed to announce the endowment. As eager as he, too, was to find more about Thomas' killer, he struggled to understand Lady Beatrix's role in the mystery. Absorbed in thought, he returned to his study. Just as he was settling into his work, the porter entered, his face clearly showing concern.

"Master," he began hesitantly, "I escorted the lady to her carriage safely, but something troubles me."

"What concerns you?"

"As Lady Beatrix left, I noticed a man observing her from behind a tree, trying to remain unseen."

"And why would that unsettle you?"

"Because, Master, I recognized him from our college. And his look showed unmistakable anger."

CHAPTER 9: TOWN-GOWN TENSIONS

In which we explore the tensions between townsfolk and scholars

It was one of those drunken nights, lately too frequent, for Gilbert of Shrewsbury. Huddled in a dim corner of the White Hart, his gaze was fixed on the liquid swirling in his pint, the ale warming his thoughts into a hazy blur. Drunken reflections of recent altercations, the undersheriff's inquiry, and incessant quarrels with his roommate swirled through his mind like mist over a fen.

Through his stupor, snippets of a nearby whisper caught his ear. "Mark ye, James, there's truth behind the Templar treasure tales."

"Truth, Hugh? Or tavern talk?" James scoffed.

"Stories have roots. I have heard lads from town have been skulking around the old manor house close by here. They reckon treasure's buried there, and they are hungry for it. They say the Templars use it for a hidey hole. They even say that there is a tunnel from St. Mary's and another from the abbey."

"Next ye'll be tellin' me there's ghosts guarding the treasure, I suppose."

"Don't ye scoff at me, James. I know what I know and ye'd best listen. There's gold to be had if ye're clever."

The rumours ignited a spark in Gilbert's muddled brain, conflating the townsmen's ambition with his own grievances. They were all usurpers – Mateld, his father, his sister, and now these townsfolk, eyeing a prize he felt was as much his by right of the university's ties to the town.

A half-remembered confrontation over similar rumours now started to seep into his ale-soaked mind, fanning the flames of resentment. Once, such whispers had seemed trivial, but now, in his ale-induced fog, he grasped their significance. He had demanded then that they divulge their secrets, sparking a confrontation that had escalated into violence.

Gilbert - Town and Gown Conflict Ignites

When Gilbert previously confronted the whisperers, their reaction was swift and brutal. They hurled him to the ground, fists and boots pounding him in a relentless assault.

"University's claim? Ye be no lord of the manor, laddie!" they jeered.

The tavern's hum turned into a cacophony as scholars and townsmen clashed, spilling into the streets where spilt ale and blood soon muddied the dirt.

Passersby, anticipating a quiet evening stroll, were caught in the growing tumult, their hue and cry summoning the undersheriff, Elric the Bald, and his constables. With swords drawn, they waded into the melee, but their arrival only intensified the battle.

Amid the chaos, a scholar, inflamed by the adrenalin of the brutal moment, brought his fist down on the head of a townsman and seized the stunned man's dagger. The weapon's theft signalled a grave turn in the fighting. New louder, more desperate shouts, rent the night air, and the metallic scent of blood scented the breeze.

As darkness encroached, the undersheriff's orders finally pierced the tumult, thinning the crowd. His deputy, spotting the armed scholar, advanced, blade at the ready.

"Enough, boy! Retreat to your cloisters," the deputy barked.

But the scholar, his robes now a banner of defiance, lunged. The dagger found its mark, and the constable crumpled to the street, his life bleeding out onto the dirt road. With his victim dying at his feet, the scholar vanished into the growing darkness.

Gilbert – Back to the Present

In the murky depths of Gilbert's mind, disjointed events tangled together: the prestigious students of Oxford flaunting their academic triumphs, the aloof townsfolk hoarding secrets of rumoured Templar treasures, the battle outside the tavern, his father's disapproval, his sister's smug satisfaction at running the family business, and Thomas, the golden boy of Balliol whose star rose too quickly to be natural.

Greta, the stout barmaid, interrupted his brooding with a clang as she slapped down another ale. "On the house, Master Gilbert. You look like you've been wrestling with ghosts."

Gilbert grunted, his stare fixated on the dark liquid which seemed to hold the reflections of his darkest thoughts. He muttered under his breath about the town's latest gossip, something about sacred treasures and ancient rights. Greta shrugged and moved on to more convivial customers.

As the ale continued to dull his senses, Gilbert's resentment seeped into every corner of his mind, filling him with a dangerous resolve. He recalled the night he had heard drunken scholars boasting of secret meetings and hidden passages beneath the university grounds, whispering of power and wealth that could change a man's fate.

The memory swam before his eyes, and for a moment, Gilbert was back there again, hidden in the shadows, his heart pounding with a mixture of excitement and rage. He had plans – plans that would show them all who he really was. He would be a fool no longer; he'd rise above the whispers and condescension. He would teach them all a lesson they never would forget.

Suddenly, Greta's laughter pierced his reverie, pulling him back to the present and the table before him with the half-empty mug. Gilbert shook his head, trying to clear the fog. His thoughts were a muddle, but one thing was crystal clear – he'd been wronged and, for that, he would have his retribution.

Something niggled at his numb brain, however. *Was it Deja vu? Had he been here before?* He recalled little of his participation in the riot, only that he woke up in his room, blood on his shirt and his roommate snoring in the bed next to his.

"It must have been a lot worse than I remembered," Gilbert mused. He must have been too close to the slaughtered constable and gotten some blood on his tunic.

Sensing that he was missing something important, Gilbert went back to sleep, not rising until the morning sun was high in the sky.

As he splashed water on his face from the basin on the table, the entry door nearby shook with thunderous knocking. Opening the door, Gilbert found himself face-to-face with Undersheriff Elric.

CHAPTER 10: A DAGGER IN THE DARKNESS

In which we trace the murder weapon and the significance it holds.

Sir Willam was having a very bad day. Returning from the burial of his son, Thomas, murdered just days before, he mused upon the missing ceremonial dagger from his collection. As a knight, he had intended to attend the funeral in full knight's regalia but his dagger, *The Mantle's Edge*, had disappeared. He recalled having worn it on the day he and Thomas exchanged words – in fact, the last time he saw Thomas – but after that he could not recall seeing it.

The Dagger – A Long and Convoluted History

The Mantel's Edge had been in Sir Willam's family for generations. Family lore suggested that it was presented to one of his forbears almost two hundred years before. What only a few of his family realized was that *The Mantel's Edge* referred to the white mantel of the Knights Templar.

Sir Willam was presented the dagger at the time of his knighting by his father, Sir Geoffrey de Shrewsbury. Sir Willam recalled the presentation vividly. Only he and his father were present in the room, the manor house's library. Sir Geoffrey placed the dagger's hilt in Willam's hand, held palm up and, reading from an ancient parchment, handed down for centuries from father to son, intoned a brief ritual:

Sir Geoffrey: *What light do we bear, my son, against the shroud of night?*

Sir Willam: *We bear the Lumen Templi, father, the secret name of this blade, the sacred light of the temple.*

Sir Geoffrey: And whence came this gleaming edge, the silent sentinel of our creed?

Sir Willam: *From the Grand Master's hand to our line, forged in piety and steeped in the blood of martyrs.*

Sir Geoffrey: *In whose honour do we sheath this blade?*

Sir Willam: *In honour of the Templar's silent vigil, and the guardianship of the cross and hidden mysteries.*

Sir Geoffrey: *And what mark does it bear, concealed from the uninitiated eye?*

Sir Willam: *It bears the crimson cross, veiled in design, a whisper of our bond to the Templar's faded glory.*

Sir Geoffrey: *To whom now do we entrust Lumen Templi, and the silent creed it carries?*

Sir Willam: *To me, the scion of our house, I take the burden and the honour, to hold fast to our silent vow.*

Sir Geoffrey: *And under what oath do you bind yourself to this legacy?*

Sir Willam: *By the sacred blood and our sacred honour, I vow to uphold the sanctity of our charge, until I pass the Lumen Templi to the next keeper of our flame.*

Sir Geoffrey: *How do you reveal the soul of Lumen Templi?*

Sir Willam: *By pressing the stone of legacy, hidden in plain sight, I unveil the ensconced cross, the heart of our Templar oath.*

Sir Geoffrey: *Press, then, the stone of legacy.*

Sir Willam recalled that he had, indeed, pressed the

stone of legacy, a pure, white diamond, set in the base of the dagger's hilt, revealing the hidden chamber within the hilt in which a carved ruby cross was set.

Sir Geoffrey: *What does the white of the stone of legacy recall?*

Sir Willam: *The white of the stone of legacy reminds us of the purity of our purpose.*

Sir Geoffrey: *And what does the crimson cross recall?*

Sir Willam: *The crimson cross reminds us of the secret and sacred duty that we hold signifying our commitment to the principles and missions of our Order.*

Sir Geoffrey: *Take, then, this blade and guard it zealously until you pass it to its next bearer.*

And Sir Geoffrey closed Willam's palm around the hit of the dagger.

The Dagger – An Unintended Journey

Walter, Sir Willam's stable boy, was hot. Very hot. It was another hot, dry day in the spring of 1295 and Walter sought the manor house with the shade and cool it promised. It had been a long, hot, strenuous day in the stables for Walter where the horses needed to be brushed down and fed.

Walter also needed to assist the farrier in repairing the iron shoes on the two huge Destrier horses the master used at tournaments and on those rare occasions when he went to battle. The four identical white Rouncies pulled the master's carriage and they, too, needed to be attended.

Tired and hot from the day's labours, Walter stealthily entered the manor house through the rear servants' entrance. Finding a cool corner by the stars leading to the first floor, Walter soon fell asleep.

Peter, the upstairs footman descended the stairs on an errand for the master and stumbled upon Walter, grabbed him by the collar and yanked him awake to his feet.

"And what would ye be doin' here, lad, instead of in the stables where ye belong?"

"I was tired and hot, Peter. I just needed a few moments of rest and cooling. I must have fallen asleep."

"You do not belong here. Don't you know the rules of the house? Stable staff never enter the house without invitation. Come, we will go find the master and see what he has to say."

Dragging Walter by his tunic collar, Peter took him before the master. Sir Willam was in the library, and, upon hearing Peter's story, he exploded with barely concealed fury.

"I will not tolerate a stable boy setting foot in this house! You have broken the rules of the manor – MY rules – and that cannot be tolerated. You are dismissed from your employment here. You have one hour to gather your possessions and leave the manor completely. Peter will see to any wages owed you and will ensure that you leave forthwith."

Sir Willam strode out of the library without looking back to summon Peter. Walter, left alone, gazed around the room, replete with trophies from glorious battles and formal occasions where Sir Willam attended, often receiving some sort of award. His eyes fixated on the ceremonial dagger – *The Mantel's Edge* – bejewelled and encased in its equally ornamented scabbard. Without a moment's hesitation, Walter drew the dagger from its scabbard and secreted it beneath his tunic just as Peter entered the room.

"Well, what are ye waitin' for, boy? Get on with ye."

"I'm leaving and I hope never to see these four walls again in all my born days." And Peter, with Walter in tow, headed towards the stables and Walter's cramped corner.

Several days passed since his abrupt dismissal and Walter's stomach growled. Without the master's recommendation, he could find no work at the nearby manor houses. Wandering aimlessly through Oxford town, he came upon a scholar walking purposefully towards a nearby tavern.

"Please, master, give me a penny that I might have something to eat. I'm hungry and have eaten nowt for these two days."

"Take your begging somewhere else, cur. I will not be giving hard-earned pennies to the likes of you. Go somewhere and work for your supper."

"What if I had something valuable to sell? Might that change your mind?"

"And what might that be? You look like a penniless stable hand to me. Where would you be getting something valuable that I might want?" As his excitement grew, the scholar's broad Irish brogue betrayed his Gaelic roots.

Withdrawing the dagger from beneath his tunic and unwrapping the cloth which concealed the blade, Walter produced the dagger. "Would this interest you?"

The scholar looked over the gleaming silver blade and, feigning disinterest, made a token offer: "I'll give you two shillings. I have no idea where you got this, but you certainly did not purchase it. Two shilling hardly pays for my risk if it is stolen."

"That won't do, master. This blade belonged to a knight, well-known in these parts. You must give more for it, risky though it may be."

"Oh, very well. I'll give you a mark for it and not a farthing more. Take it or leave it."

Agreeing, Walter wrapped the blade up again and handed it to the scholar who passed over the promised coins. Walter hurried away and was not seen again.

The scholar, new prize hidden in the billowing sleeve of his gown, hurried back to his room at the college. As he passed through the hall doors, he noted a game of dice in the common room. "Hmm… a chance to recoup what I paid for this blade and more." And he entered the room. "Room for one more?"

"We always are glad to take your money. Come in and take a seat. The dice run favourable."

It was not the scholar's day to win, however. After a few rolls of the dice, he was out of money.

"I'm in for another roll, lads."

"Not without money, you're not."

The scholar thought for a moment and pulled out the dagger from the sleeve of his gown.

"How about this, then. I'll wager it against the entire pot. I got it from a knight, well-known hereabouts."

The eyes of his opponents grew large, and one of the gamblers gasped aloud.

The young man holding the dice exclaimed, "I don't know about the rest of you, but I'm in. I'll put all I have in the pot and you," eying the scholar, "put in the blade."

The scholar did so. As he did, the other players put their money in as well. The dice rolled. And, for the scholar, they rolled badly.

The gambler who had accepted the scholar's challenge looked at him with a smirking grin. "Bad luck me lad. I'll take the blade, the pot, and be gone while I'm ahead."

Before he knew it the blade was gone. All that was left to the scholar was to retreat to his cramped room and seek respite from his defeat.

Sir Willam – Discovery

Sir Willam sat in his overstuffed leather chair in the library mulling over his recent tiff with his son, his death, the dismissal of the stable boy and the general run of bad fortune in which he found himself. It had been several days since he had returned to the comforts of the library. It was his favourite room, and it housed his most precious treasures.

Sir Willam let his eyes roam over the nick-knacks and trophies scattered amongst books on the shelves. His gaze rested upon the empty scabbard that once held the *Lumen Templi*, secret name of the *Mantel's Edge*.

The dagger was gone.

CHAPTER II: THE WHISPERING DEAD

In which we observe the killer's paranoia begin to surface, fearing retribution from beyond the grave and Isabel's vision comes to life.

Thomas's killer lay in his bed, restlessness consuming him. Sleep, a stranger since the murder, eluded him again this night. In his dreams, Thomas's spectre haunted him relentlessly.

"You caused my death, and I will have my revenge," the apparition declared.

"You're not real. You're not Thomas. Why do you haunt me?" he murmured into the darkness, though he expected no answer. Yet, the spirit repeated its ominous vow, "You caused my death, and I will have my revenge."

Denial was his shield. "You will not have your revenge, Thomas. You're nothing but a figment, a spectre conjured by indigestion, surely." But the ten words echoed back at him, unyielding.

Another night passed, sleepless. Whispers had reached him that the murder weapon had been discovered. *Or was it merely a ruse, the undersheriff's tactic, to push him towards confession?* The pudding he had for supper did have an odd taste. Yes, that must be it—just the undersheriff's trickery and some bad pudding.

But sleep did not come. Thomas's spectral accusations looped endlessly in his mind.

The Killer – More Dreams

The killer tossed in his bed. In his dream, he felt the jolts and bumps of the wagon as it bounced along, empty, past Oxford Town.

He recalled leaving town, heading towards Rewley Abbey for his secret rendezvous with Thomas. Night was falling, and he could not afford to be late, nor did he wish to encounter Thomas on the way.

He had heard the farmer's wagon approaching and swiftly ducked into a shadow. It was clear that the farmer was returning to his farm with an empty wagon after providing forage for his cattle in the field. The hot, dry spring had made it challenging for the cows to find such forage, the grass in the fields slow growing.

As the wagon passed the killer's hiding place, he silently jumped aboard and lay flat, determined to stay hidden. The wagon continued to bounce along and the killer, troubled by the dream, tossed and turned on the hard, straw-filled mattress. Sleep eluded him, and he drifted in and out of the dream.

Suddenly, the killer was wide awake. *Had he seen someone lurking alongside the road?* It could not be possible; he was alone, concealed in the shadows. There could not be a lurker. It was impossible. The killer found himself sweating in the hot night air.

No, there was no lurker. He was safe. There was no clandestine watcher in the darkness.

But there was...

The Killer – Wystan the Sage

With the dawn, the sky hung heavy, with gray clouds threatening another day of suffocating heat. The killer knew he was haunted, not just by dreams, but by the relentless spirit of Thomas. *To whom could he turn? Whom could he trust?*

Dressing wearily, he abandoned any pretence of attending classes, his mind a whirlpool of fatigue and confusion. He wandered aimlessly across the college lawns until he found himself at the Balliol Postern and Old Cedric, the porter.

"Out for a stroll, then?" Cedric inquired.

"No. Troubled, Cedric. Troubled by nightmares I cannot seem to escape," he confessed.

"Ah, you need to see Wystan, the Sage. A former priest, he is. Wise in these matters, and very discreet, he will be."

"And where might I find this Wystan?"

"Cross the river from the town gate, walk about a mile, and you'll find yourself at a crossroads. His abode is there —a large stone house, impossible to miss. There is nowt nearby."

Somewhat sceptical, the killer set off as Old Cedric directed him. The house at the crossroads loomed large and imposing, an ancient manor brooding with secrets. The crossroads disturbed the killer. Crossroads were a place of evil. Some said they were a place of devils and evil spirits.

The killer hesitated, trying to decide whether he wanted to go up to the door of the house and, he mused, tempt fate. A nudge pushed him toward the ancient building, one incapable of resisting. As he approached the door, full of apprehension, it opened wide, revealing a wizened old man in a monk's cowl and hood.

"Are you Master Wystan?"

"No. I am his servant. But, come. He is expecting you. I will take you to him."

Puzzled, the killer followed the servant. *How could Master Wystan possibly be expecting him if he hadn't even decided himself but an hour or so ago?* He prepared himself for a frightening encounter, but when the door to Master Wystan's work room opened, the killer saw a man, ancient in visage with a white flowing beard and huge, drooping moustache. He was dressed much as his servant in a monk's cowl and hood. The expression on his face was, decidedly, one of wisdom and kindness.

"No," the killer decided, "there seems nothing to fear here. But there may be no respite from my dreams either. We will see."

The Killer – Master Wystan Speaks

"My son, you are troubled."

"Yes, Master Wystan, but how could you know that? Have you spoken of me to old Cedric?"

"No. Old Cedric is a wise, canny man, knowledgeable in the ways of the world, but never have we spoken of you." And he said the killer's name.

"But then, how could you possibly know?"

"It is my way to know when someone is troubled. I feel it in the tides of time, the whispers of the breeze, the voices of the animals, the movements of the stars. You are having dreams of something that you did. Something very bad. Something for which you will, one day, pay dearly."

"I don't believe you. Someone has told you.... You cannot possibly know..."

"Shall I tell you what you did, boy? Yes, I shall. Then you will believe. You murdered Thomas of Hereford in cold blood."

The killer's knees weakened. He felt that he would collapse in shock on the Mage's straw-covered floor. But Master Wystan's old servant came to his rescue and guided him to a hard, straight-back wooden chair where he offered the killer some water.

"But what can I do? The dreams…"

"You are troubled by a demon of Saturn, and you must implore one of his archangels to protect you."

"But how can I do that, Master? I know nothing of such things."

"No matter. I will do it for you. For a price, of course."

"But what price, Master. I have nothing. I am a poor scholar."

"I will tell you in good time. But you must agree that when I tell you, you will pay my price without argument, deceit, or resistance."

"Yes, yes! If you or your archangels can stop the dreams, I will pay your price if it is within my ability to do so."

"Fine. Now you must go away and not return until the next full moon. Then, at midnight, you will meet me at the crossroads, and I will give you an amulet that will protect you."

"But what is this amulet, Master? I know nothing of amulets or magic."

"Never mind for now. I will tell you all as well as how to use the amulet, but now, you must go. Until the next full moon, then…" And Master Wystan was gone as if he never had been there.

Was this a dream? Some cruel trick of Old Cedric? As he was standing in the middle of the straw-covered workroom, shivering with cold even though it was very warm outside, Master Wystan's servant approached. "Come, lad, I will take you back to the road."

And before he knew what was happening, the killer was at the crossroads, walking slowly toward Oxford Town, trance-like.

Master Wystan's servant was nowhere to be seen.

Master Wystan – A Ritual of Protection

Wystan, the Sage, was in his workroom with his servant. He stood within a mystical circle of protection, carved into the rough wood floor a design he had learned from ancient scrolls during his travels. The circle protected the mage from malevolent forces. An adjacent triangle served as a boundary to contain summoned spirits until he could safely dismiss them. Master Wystan was well-versed in the arcane arts and guarded his secrets carefully, knowing the potential consequences were they ever misused.

His servant took a piece of lead, skilfully shaping it into a perfect circle. Using a burin, a knife designed for engraving, he carefully carved the intricate design of the Second Pentacle of Saturn onto the lead disk. This pentacle was considered powerful in warding off adversaries.

Stepping into the magic circle, the servant offered the lead disk to Master Wystan. The Hebrew characters inscribed upon the disk possessed profound mystical significance, their combined numerical value of 26 held a sacred connection to the name of God.

Master Wystan began the ritual by invoking the safeguards of the magic circle. He then extended the lead disk to each of the four cardinal directions, accompanying the gesture with a solemn incantation. As he chanted, the characters etched on the disk began to emit a brilliant, fiery glow.

With deliberate care, the mage passed the disk through the incense coming from the censor positioned at the western boundary of the circle. The disk burst into flames, only for the flames to dissipate in an instant.

Finally, Master Wystan placed the enchanted amulet within a small walnut box and exited the magic circle, placing the small wooden box on his worktable. The box's lid was sealed shut with a single drop of lead, securing the amulet's mystical power.

The Killer – The Mage and the Crossroads

It was precisely midnight when the killer reached the crossroads. The full moon, in a cloudless night sky, bathed the area in its silvery light, making it appear almost like daytime. However, the killer stood alone. The mage had not yet appeared, but a small walnut wood box rested at the exact centre of the crossroads.

The killer found no restful sleep since his last encounter in this eerie place. He vividly recalled his unsettling conversation with Master Wystan, and a shiver ran down his spine. His gaze fixed upon the box. *Should he dare to discover its contents?* He started to reach for it but before he could pick it up, the mage's commanding voice halted his movements.

"Do not!" the voice echoed, and the killer froze. He turned and saw Master Wystan approaching from his nearby dwelling.

The moon hung overhead, casting no discernible shadows. Armed with a sword, the mage intoned a prayer in

Latin for the sword's protective powers:

Ego te conjuro, o gladius, per haec nomina Abrahach, Abrach, Abracadabra, Yod He Vau He, ut mihi serviatur in virtute et defensione in omnibus operationibus magicis, contra omnes inimicos meos visibiles et invisibiles.

With the magical sword in hand, he drew a large circle surrounding the small box, himself, and the killer at the centre of the crossroads. Using a knife with a black handle, Master Wystan inscribed mystical characters within and around the circle, never stepping outside of it. At the western edge of the circle, he placed a censer filled with fragrant incense. The passing of his hand over the censer ignited the incense, releasing a heavy, pungent aroma.

The mage then removed the amulet from the box and passed the lead disk, bearing the same symbols as those inscribed within and around the circle, through the fragrant incense smoke tapping it three times—the magical number of Saturn—with his wand. He intoned the charge of the amulet in the service of Saturn's angel, Maymon: "Maymon, protector of lost souls, lend your strength to this vessel."

Next, in Latin, he invoked the demon Cafziel in the service of Saturn and Maymon: *"Venire ad me, Cafziel, daemonium Saturni. Tu vincitur a Maymon."*

As in his workroom, the amulet began to glow with a white-hot fire. Master Wystan placed the amulet in the killer's right hand and closed the hand around the leaden disk. The killer screamed in pain, attempting to drop the amulet, but he could not open his hand.

Then, as swiftly as it had begun, the pain in the killer's hand subsided. He cautiously opened his hand and gazed in astonishment and shock. The symbols on the amulet were burned onto his hand.

"What have you done to me?" the killer cried out.

"This binding shields against your adversaries, both in the physical world and the spiritual realm. You are safeguarded by the archangel Maymon and his servant Cafziel. As long as you wear this amulet around your neck, suspended by a silver chain, no harm shall befall you. Silver is the metal of the moon. It offers added protection."

"But what if I lose the amulet, Master? What then?"

"Should you lose it or fail to fulfil the payment, I shall demand when the time comes, all protection shall be lost, and you shall once again be at the mercy of Thomas and his demonic cohorts."

Before the killer could respond, the mage, the box, and the circle vanished. The killer placed the charged amulet around his neck on its silver chain. Feeling bewildered and disoriented, he began his journey back toward Oxford town. Doubt crept into his thoughts. "Did this truly happen?" he pondered. However, the tangible proof rested around his neck and was etched into his hand.

The gates of Oxford town had long been sealed shut, and the killer did not wish to alert the town's watchmen. Spotting a small copse of trees by the roadside, he drew his cloak tightly around him and sought refuge amidst the shelter of the hedgerows and trees. There, he descended into a deep slumber, undisturbed until morning.

Isabel – Rosamunde Speaks

Isabel, the novice, was haunted by dreams of the long-deceased Rosamunde. Every night, as Isabel drifted into slumber, a vision of Rosamunde materialized, sitting on her bier and pointing directly at Isabel. Each time, she seemed on the verge of uttering something, but Isabel would awaken before any words could escape her lips.

Except for the last time.

On that occasion, Rosamunde did speak, and Isabel was gripped by terror.

"Isabel, you have sinned! You have transgressed the Lord's commandment. You must confess your sin and seek forgiveness."

The voice was sepulchral, paralyzing Isabel with fear. She struggled to wake up, but her efforts were in vain. Rosamunde continued, "You have aided a man in his death. The Lord commands, 'Thou shalt not kill,' yet you have done so, just as if you had delivered the fatal blow."

Isabel remained frozen, unable to move or awaken. She could not respond.

"Isabel... seek out your confessor. Confess your sin. Perform acts of contrition. Accept your punishment."

With that, Rosamunde reclined on her bier, and Isabel awoke, drenched in a cold sweat.

The following evening, exhaustion overwhelmed Isabel from a strenuous day's work. Nevertheless, she resisted sleep, fearing a recurrence of the previous night's torment. Eventually, fatigue overcame her, and she succumbed to slumber. But Rosamunde did not return.

In fact, Rosamunde never visited Isabel's dreams again.

CHAPTER 12: UNLIKELY ALLIES

In which Sister Agnes gains unexpected allies in her investigation.

OLD Cedric sat at a table in a quiet corner of the Black Swan Tavern. It was his only day of rest, the other six being spent guarding the Balliol Postern. When he had this rare respite from the labours of protecting the college, he preferred the company of a good cup of ale and whatever the tavern had on offer as food.

Today had been exceptionally fortunate; the tavern served an aromatic lamb stew. The slow-stewed lamb with onions, garlic, and herbs of which only the landlord knew, made the pottage particularly inviting. Cedric took a draught of his ale and contemplated the fragrance of the steaming bowl, almost reluctant to disturb its pungent odour. "But," he thought, "one must eat, fragrance or no."

As he ate, he noticed an immense knight entering the tavern. He was exceptionally tall, strongly built, his golden, flowing hair peeking out from beneath his helmet. He had a profuse golden beard and huge drooping moustache. He wore the tell-tale scarlet cross of the Knights Templar. All eyes in the tavern were on him as he walked towards the bar. Cedric noticed, as did the rest of the patrons, that the knight was alone. He also noted that he never had seen the knight before.

"Do come and join me Sir Knight. Although the days have been exceptionally warm, the nights can be quite cool, and I have an excellent seat by the fire."

"I will join you." The accent was strange, not quite Norse, not quite French, and not quite English.

"Mateld! Come see to this noble Knight Templar! I sense that he has travelled far and is in need of sustenance!"

Mateld, the barmaid, made a small curtsy, "How may I serve you, Sir Knight? We have a lovely lamb stew, which Old Cedric here already has devoured."

"Barmaid, I would have a jug of mead and, yes, the lamb seems quite satisfactory, so I'll have that as well."

The knight removed his helmet and settled into the straight-backed wooden chair at Old Cedric's table.

"Have you travelled far? Perhaps returning from the Crusades?"

"Yes. I just have returned from the Holy Land and am joining my troop here in Oxfordshire after accompanying some important documents to Templar authorities. And who might you be, old man?"

"Oh, people around here just call me 'Old Cedric.' I guard the Balliol Postern and today is my day of rest. How are you called, Sir Knight?"

"I am Eric du Nordsk. My father was a noble Viking warrior. He was in a raiding party, and he left it to wed an English maiden of French descent."

"I note your accent. I assume that it is a mixture of English, French and, perhaps, Norwegian?"

"You assume correctly, Old Man. We spoke all three in my household as I grew up."

Old Cedric – The Knight's Tale

Mateld delivered the food and drink to the knight. "Another jug of mead, wench!"

"Of course, Sir Knight. Right away." Another small curtsy. Mateld was smitten. She could not take her eyes off the huge, handsome knight. "But," she recalled, "there would be none of his affection for me. His vows of chastity and celibacy would prevent me even getting his attention beyond my chores in the tavern. But still…" her thoughts trailed off and she went to fetch the mead.

The knight's pale blue eyes pieced Old Cedric to his soul. Sternly, he asked, "You know everyone in Oxford Town, do you not, Old Man?"

"Well, almost everybody. Sometimes there are strangers in town–just such as you–and there are some who simply are passing through on their way to somewhere else. But mostly I know the folks around here. Why do you ask?"

"I would tell you a tale, Old Man, and perhaps, you can tell me of someone who can advise me." His eyes never flinched, never blinked as he stared at Old Cedric.

Speaking less formal now, Old Cedric replied, "I certainly will try, Sir Eric. Speak your story."

The knight began his tale, his eyes not wavering from the deep stare into Cedric's.

"As I told you, I am returning from the Holy Land with important documents for my superiors. I was directed to go to a large manor house outside of town. I came to the crossroads, and there, off to the side of one of the roads stood a large manor house such as was described to me in my instructions.

As the hour approached midnight, the moon still shone full and bright. I tethered my war horse well off the road and settled down behind some bushes for a night of rest before addressing the household in the mansion. As I was preparing for rest, I heard a commotion in the road. I crawled quietly to where I could observe without being observed.

When I looked out, I saw an old man in a monk's cowl drawing something in the dirt of the crossroads. Next the old man withdrew a small object from the sleeve of his cloak and placed it on the ground in the middle of the crossroads. Finally, he took a large censer from his pack, set it up, filled it with incense and paused as if waiting for someone."

"And did someone come?"

"Yes. A young man in a scholar's cloak and hood."

"And did you see this lad? Could you describe him?"

"No. Even with the bright moonlight the newcomer never faced my hiding place until the end but even so, he was too covered by the hood of his cloak."

"Pray continue with your story, Sir Eric."

"I could see that the lad was partially overcome by the fumes from the censer. He staggered when he walked and when he spoke, his speech slurred somewhat. Then the old man began an incantation of some sort and picked up the wooden box which he had removed from the sleeve of his cloak and placed on the ground.

Having picked up the box, and with more incantations, he opened it and withdrew a small, black metallic disk. This he placed in the scholar's hand. The scholar screamed with pain but, apparently, the pain subsided rapidly for his cries ceased as quickly as they had started.

By this time, the scholar was so overcome by the incense that he lay down in the middle of the crossroads, appearing to sleep. The old man in the monk's cowl swept the dirt road clear of the symbols that he had carved with his sword and flung the small box in my direction. Of course, I was not observed in all of this.

When the old man had finished, he collected the censer and returned to the mansion. The young man awoke, looking confused and he started towards town, but a half mile or so on he, probably realizing that it would not be easy to enter the town at this late hour, crawled behind a hedge as I had done and fell fast asleep. I, after a brief search, found the box. And here it is."

"Obviously, you witnessed a magical ritual of some sort, and this box was part of it. I know of a person who could advise you in this matter, but you must trust her."

"That I happily would do. There is something about this box that discomforts me. I would be rid of it."

"And were you observed?"

"Perhaps. I cannot be sure. As I said, the young scholar stared at me in my hiding place very briefly, but I am quite sure that he did not see me."

"Well, when you are finished here, you must go to the convent and ask for Sister Agnes. She is the infirmarist, so she likely will be available at this time of day. Give her the box and tell her your story. She is wise and will advise you well. Of that, I am certain."

"That, I will do, Cedric, and gladly." He quaffed the last of his mead, replaced the box in his sleeve pocket, picked up his helmet and, with a nod of thanks to Old Cedric, left the tavern. Mateld's eyes, wide as a new fawn, stared after him with longing.

Sir Eric – Revelations

The Templar mounted his horse and headed for the main gate to the city. There he drew the attention of the warden guarding the gate.

"Warden… direct me to the convent."

Pointing forward, the warden directed him. "Travel down this road until you reach the bridge that spans the Thames. Cross over the bridge, and then continue along Abbey Road until you arrive at the convent. May God be with you on your quest."

"Thank you, Warden, and with you, as well."

Sir Eric followed the warden's instructions and, before long, reached the Abbey. A young novice designated as the warden at the time met him at the abbey gate.

"I would meet with Sister Agnes on a matter of some urgency and secrecy."

"Please wait here at the gate, Sir Knight, and I shall enquire of the Mother Superior as to how to admit you."

Moments later the novice and the prioress returned to the gate.

"Sir Knight, I will guide you to the convent garden where you may meet with Sister Agnes in privacy. However, I shall remain with you and Sister Agnes as our rules of propriety dictate."

"Thank you, Mother, I shall be honoured by your presence."

The prioress and Sir Eric arrived at the garden, a quiet, restful collection of flowers, shade trees and an herb garden kept by Sister Agnes for her herbal remedies and poultices. Shortly after they reached a stone bench, places in the garden, as accommodation for sisters who wanted to sit quietly and contemplate the Lord and His creation.

The prioress sat and the novice accompanying them moved off to the side out of earshot. Sister Agnes arrived shortly thereafter and sat beside the prioress.

"Sir Knight, what is it that we may do to ease your

burden?"

"Sister Agnes, I have a strange tale to tell, and Old Cedric tells me that I must tell it to you."

"Well, Sir Knight, pray tell us your story. Mother and I are anxious to hear it in all its detail."

The knight recounted his story exactly as he had told it to Old Cedric, ending by producing the small black box from the sleeve of his tunic. At once, both Agnes and the Prioress recoiled.

"That is a very dangerous artefact, Sir Knight. We must summon our priest and confessor to help us before we go any further." Both women refused to touch the box.

"I agree, Mother. I will attend his coming before I go on."

Agnes summoned the young novice who approached the group shyly, for this was an eminent group, including as it did, the Mother Superior, Sister Agnes, and the Knight Templar. For a moment, the novice forgot that she was in training for the taking of her vows and, like Mateld, gaped at the huge, handsome knight. The moment passed quickly.

"How may I serve you, Sisters?"

"Please go to the chapel and ask the confessor to join us here on a matter of some importance."

"Yes, Mother. I shall fetch him at once." And she was off. It was not long before she reappeared with the aged priest and, seeing that the eyes of the assembly were on him, retreated to her spot out of hearing until she might again be summoned.

"Father, thank you for coming so quickly. This knight has brought us a strange story along with a small box which may be cursed."

"I certainly will respond to the summons of one so

worthy as you, Mother. Now what is this tale?" Again, the knight recounted his experiences at the crossroads concluding with the removal of the box from his tunic sleeve. The priest examined it closely, without touching it.

"What is the significance of this artefact, Mother?"

"I shall ask Sister Agnes to explain, Father."

"Very well. Sister?"

"From all that the knight told us, I do believe this box once contained an amulet, prepared by Wystan the Sage, intended to protect the man whom I suspect of murdering Thomas of Hereford these few weeks ago. It suggests that the killer is tormented by guilt for his actions and has sought supernatural assistance to shield himself from the demons that Master Wystan convinced him are causing his distress.

This knight has recounted a tale that implies that Wystan, using noxious fumes from a censer, convinced the killer that the former contents of this box would provide protection. It may be deceit, or the box and the amulet might be cursed. We do not have certainty, but before I commence my analysis, I implore God's protection."

"Then let us proceed to the chapel, Sister, and I shall conduct an exorcism and blessing to ensure your safety as you undertake the Lord's work to uncover the perpetrator of this heinous crime."

The group departed from the tranquil garden, passing into the abbey chapel. Upon their arrival, the elderly priest led them to a large font filled with holy water at the rear of the nave. He blessed each person and then took the box from the knight. Sprinkling the small box with holy water from the font, he intoned a protective prayer, concluding with "*Gloria Patri et Filio et Spiritui Sancto.*"

Next, there was a renunciation of evil for Sister Agnes,

the prioress, and the knight, followed by an exorcism prayer, both for the box and for the knight who had possessed it for the past two days. The priest then blessed the box, praying that it would be used for holy purposes in the quest to uncover Thomas's killer.

He concluded by dismissing any malevolent spirits from the box, adjuring them to return to their origins and never return. The elderly priest prayed for God's peace to fill the space once occupied by the demons conjured by Master Wystan, and thus the ritual ended.

The group departed, splitting up to go their separate ways and Agnes, box in hand, returned to her workroom.

CHAPTER 13: SEEDS OF DOUBT

In which we are introduced to skeptical and obstructive forces, both within and outside the convent.

Sister Agnes placed the small wooden box on her worktable and summoned her novice, Isabel.

"Isabel, please come with your writing utensils. I will need detailed notes of this examination."

"Yes, Sister. I am on my way." Isabel entered the workroom with quills, ink, and parchment in hand. She sat down at one of the smaller worktables near the head of Agnes' table and arranged her tools. She was ready to record.

No sooner had Isabel settled than another novice entered the room. "Sister, Lady Beatrix is outside with Mother Alice, Proctor Stonehand, and the undersheriff. They request an audience with you."

Sister Agnes – Official Resistance to Her Investigation

"By all means, Sister, invite them in." Sister Agnes could not imagine why this delegation was visiting her so soon after she had returned from the exorcism. She had little time to speculate. The Prioress came straight to the point.

"There are concerns about your investigation, Sister. Undersheriff Alric and Proctor Stonehand do not agree with your involvement in this examination."

"And why is that, Mother?" Agnes was confused but

retained her composure.

"They believe that this is the duty of officially appointed law enforcement officers. The role of the undersheriff is, I think, obvious. Proctor Stonehand is here to represent the interests of the university."

Lady Beatrix broke into the conversation gently. "Sirs, may I have a word?"

"Of course, my lady." The undersheriff was cautious. Lady Beatrix's family held considerable influence in Oxfordshire.

"Sheriff and Proctor Stonehand, I am working closely with Sister Agnes, and we have made significant progress toward a solution. Sister Agnes possesses remarkable skills for unravelling the mysteries surrounding these tragic events. She has conducted intricate examinations of the deceased, delving into the intricacies of anatomy to provide insights into the causes of death. Her attention to detail and ability to link the murder weapon to a shard found within the victim's body demonstrate her profound understanding of these matters. Her expertise extends beyond the ordinary, and her contributions are invaluable in helping us find the truth."

At first, the two officials appeared unmoved. Then the Prioress entered the conversation, "Sirs, Sister Agnes has the knowledge, tools, and experience to perform meticulous examinations in this matter, as she has proven. You would do well to take advantage of her expertise if you wish to solve this murder quickly. With God's help, Sister Agnes and Lady Beatrix may be able to help you bring this to a speedy conclusion."

Immediately, both men's expressions changed from defiance to caution.

The sheriff cleared his throat and addressed Lady

Beatrix, "You are working with Sister Agnes on this murder, my lady?"

"Yes. She and I are dedicated to finding the truth. My family is an ardent supporter of the abbey, particularly Sister Agnes."

This declaration had an effect on the two men. Lady Beatrix hailed from a powerful family, and they did not wish to antagonize them. However, they remained unconvinced, even though it was clear that they needed to find some middle ground. Besides, Beatrix was right. The nun possessed advanced skills that could assist them.

The undersheriff turned to the Prioress, "Mother Alice, will you oversee this work to ensure that we receive all the information uncovered by Lady Beatrix and Sister Agnes?"

"I will. Sister Agnes maintains detailed notes of her procedures and results, and I will ensure that you both receive copies of those notes. I will also ensure that the evidence she uncovers is retained safely, so that when you bring the case to trial, you will have everything you need. I trust that will be satisfactory." It was not a question, and both men recognized that the conversation had concluded.

The undersheriff was somewhat contrite as he and the proctor prepared to leave. "Very well, Mother. That will be satisfactory. But we are counting on you to keep this investigation progressing in the right direction."

"The right direction, sirs, is the solution of the crime and the prosecution of the killer. With God's help, we will achieve those objectives. Good day to you, Sheriff, and Proctor." The novice who had accompanied the visitors moved away to guide them to the abbey gate.

When they had gone, the Prioress addressed both Sister Agnes and Lady Beatrix, her voice firm but not harsh, "You will conduct this investigation quickly, thoroughly, and correctly. You will maintain detailed notes, and you will retain and safeguard all physical evidence. Is this understood?"

"Of course, Mother. But you sound concerned. May I ask why?" Sister Agnes was apprehensive.

"This has become very political, Sister. The abbey prefers to withdraw from the politics of men and remain aligned with the will of God. However, I am satisfied that we can do both if we proceed with caution." And the Prioress left the room, leaving Agnes and Beatrix looking at each other with no little trepidation.

Sister Agnes – The Examination of the Box

First, Sister Agnes took parchment, quill, and ink and drew a detailed sketch of the box. She examined the box carefully with the magnifying stone to ensure that she had copied every scratch or imperfection. Sprinkling fine sand on her drawing to make certain that the ink did not smear and make parts of the drawing unreadable, she set the drawing aside for safe keeping.

Examining both the interior and exterior of the box with the magnifying stone, Agnes was surprised to see a small, almost invisible, latch on the interior of the box. Taking a small metal pick, she manipulated the latch until it caused a secret compartment to spring open. Taking a candle, she examined the compartment.

"Look you, Sister Isabel. There is a small hidden compartment in the box, and it appears to contain a small piece of parchment with drawings upon it. Please record this carefully." She took a small brush and brushed away the dust on the ancient parchment, making the writing on it clearer. Using tweezers, she then gently removed the parchment and opened it to examine its strange inscription.

But there was no inscription for her to read. Rather, to her bewilderment, there was only a simple drawing scrawled on the black parchment. "Isabel, make a careful drawing of this parchment and describe in detail how we came by it. I am going to seek the answer to what this drawing represents."

Sister Agnes entered the abbey's scriptorium. Sister Abagail, an elderly nun who had been the abbey's Scriptorix for as long as Agnes could recall, met her at the entrance. "Welcome, Sister. How may I serve you?"

"I have discovered a small parchment in a box that I suspect was somehow involved with the killing of Thomas the lecturer. Do you have a manuscript or volume that could help me identify it?"

"Let me see it, please, Sister. I will see what I can do." Abagail examined the drawing done by Agnes, turning it in every direction. "Sister, this is a heretical drawing. From my limited study of such forbidden arts, I would say that this is the sigil of some angel, probably intended for use as protection. Let us consult a manuscript that I have exactly for this purpose. Because it is so dangerous even to possess such knowledge, this is the only such manuscript I have. It was donated by one of the monks at Rewley Abbey."

The two nuns walked through the large scriptorium, passing sisters engrossed in the study of beautiful illuminated religious manuscripts. In the back of the room, under a pile of manuscripts, Abagail pulled out a small booklet with several pages. Taking the drawing again, Sister Abagail thumbed through the pages of the manuscript until she stopped at a drawing that looked identical to the one Sister Agnes had handed to her.

"Look, Sister Agnes. Here is your drawing with the description: *'Sigil Cafziel, famulus Saturni, munit contra malos angelos, qui somnum perturbant et timorem faciunt.'* ('The sigil of Cafziel, servant of Saturn, gives protection against evil angels that trouble the sleep and cause fear.')."

"This is most interesting, Sister. It implies that the killer, perhaps, is haunted by the recollection of his crime and has sought supernatural assistance in recovering from his fear."

"I am glad that I could help you, Sister Agnes. This is a rare manuscript, and we have no others of this type in the abbey. I fear keeping this knowledge within our cloisters is inviting evil."

"Thank you, Sister Abagail. God go with you," and Agnes left the scriptorium.

Sister Agnes – Mother Superior's Concern

When Agnes returned to her workroom, she found the Mother Superior waiting for her.

"What a surprise, Mother! Is there something new since our meeting?"

"Indeed, there is, Sister. I am concerned about the path this investigation is taking. Sister Abagail came quick and spoke to me about your visit."

"Mother, I just left her scriptorium. What can be her concern?"

"She is uncomfortable with your interest in heretical manuscripts. She believes that your investigation invites evil into our midst."

"I understand Mother. However, I simply needed to

identify the drawing on the parchment that I removed from the black box. Look. It is a sigil of protection. If the young scholar that the Templar Knight observed at the crossroads was the killer, it appears that he is suffering serious pangs of conscience and has sought supernatural help through Master Wystan."

"Then we must identify the young man at the crossroads, Sister Agnes, and bring this to a conclusion before other sisters become concerned and resist these activities within our walls."

"I understand, Mother. I will continue as rapidly as I can, and I will keep a low profile from now on."

"Thank you, Sister. Was cannot afford rebellion in the Abbey. We are a holy order, and we must remember that at all times."

Before Sister Agnes could respond, the Mother Superior turned and left the workroom without further comment.

CHAPTER 14: CHASING SHADOWS

In which we observe the killer's attempts to mislead the investigation.

The killer grew increasingly convinced that he had been discovered. Master Wystan's charm seemingly had worked well during the nights, but as the day wore on, waves of guilt and panic washed over him.

He needed to find a way to disrupt the undersheriff's investigation. Several strategies crossed his mind. Mayhap he could fabricate a false alibi, with the help of a friend at the *White Hart*. However, needing an alibi would only raise suspicion.

The more he pondered, the more he became certain that shifting the blame onto someone else was the answer. Finding a suitable scapegoat should not be too difficult. What he did not realize was that, unintentionally, someone else was already implicating themselves.

The Killer – The Dagger and the Scholar

Recalling that he had stolen a dagger from a scholar who had won it in a game of dice, the killer devised a plan to point the finger at the scholar as the murderer. He hastily wrote a note and called upon a friend.

"Take this note to Godstow Abbey and inform Sister Isabel, a novice there, that it is for her. Do not delay; this is of utmost importance."

Upon receiving the note, Isabel felt a sense of unease. It instructed, "Meet me tonight after Compline by the abbey wall."

There was no signature, but the message was clear. She was once again being drawn into the web of deceit surrounding the murder of Thomas the lecturer. "But Thomas is already dead," she mused. "What more could anyone possibly want of me?"

Nevertheless, shortly after the abbey bell rang to signal the end of Compline, Isabel moved discreetly towards the hidden door in the abbey wall, leading to the outside. Many of the nuns either remained unaware of the secret door, hidden within the gardens tended by the novice, or chose not to speak of it. This was not Isabel's first clandestine meeting through this passage, but tonight she was especially cautious, haunted by the memory of *The Fair Rosamund*'s ominous warnings.

In the shadows by the abbey wall, the killer awaited. He whispered, "You must tell your friend Lady Beatrix that you heard the murder weapon came from a scholar at Baliol who won it in a game of dice," and he spoke the scholar's name. "Do not fail me in this. I possess the means to reach you, and your life will hold no value if you do."

Isabel trembled with fear. Without uttering another word, she slipped back into the abbey through the concealed door. "What am I to do?" she agonized. She found herself complicit in Thomas's death, and now she was being coerced into lying to shield the killer, potentially implicating an innocent person in the process. Dread for the fate of her eternal soul weighed heavily on Isabel's mind.

Undersheriff Alric the Bald – Following a Clue

It was not long before Isabel found the opportunity to speak with Lady Beatrix. "My lady, I have heard a rumour, and it is disturbing."

"Sister, what have you heard that disturbs you so?"

There is a rumour that a scholar won a bejewelled dagger in a game of dice at Baliol."

"And how came you by this rumour, Sister?"

"One of the delivery boys from town mentioned it when he made his delivery yesterday. I was in the pantry when he delivered his goods."

"It is not good to spread this type of rumour, Sister Isabel. It can cause unrest. However, I will mention it to Sister Agnes. Thank you, Sister, and, please, be a bit more discrete."

"Certainly, my lady. Thank you." And Isabel left quietly.

Beatrix mulled the information over in her mind, wondering what credence it might have, if any, for their investigation. She decided that it would be for Agnes to decide, and she headed for Sister Agnes' workroom.

"Good day to you Sister."

"And to you as well, my lady. To what do I owe the pleasure of your company this lovely morning?"

"I came by to see what progress, Sister, and I was met by your novice. She relayed a rumour from the town that she heard from a delivery boy."

"I must speak with Isabel. Delivery boys from town have no business with her, and she should keep to her duties. In any event, we have this rumour, whether true or false. Pray, what is it?"

"It appears that a scholar from Baliol was gambling at dice, and he won a bejewelled dagger. I cannot verify the truth of it. My presence at the college would rouse suspicions, and I likely would learn nothing."

"I agree, my lady. You might seek out the undersheriff

and relay the rumour to him. I am certain that he will look into it. Besides, we have promised him that we would bring him anything that we learned. So, do you seek him out and tell him the delivery boy's tale."

Beatrix paused, thoughtfully. "Sister, do you suppose that this rumour might yield the killer of Thomas?"

Agnes contemplated the question for a moment before she replied, "I don't know my lady. Rumours of this type are of ill repute, as well you, yourself, know. Let us not put too much store in it just yet. The undersheriff will find out."

Beatrix left the abbey and headed for the undersheriff's shire house. The office was in a low, two-story building of timber and stone. The outer walls were whitewashed, and the windows were barred. Inside, the shire house contained the undersheriff's work room on the first floor and living quarters on the second. A small gaol was attached to the rear of the building with accommodation for prisoners being held before trial and the guard when the gaol was occupied.

As she approached the centre of town and the shire house, Beatrix paused. She considered the efficacy of a direct visit. Should the rumour prove true, it might be used in court and written evidence would be important. Determined to ensure that the evidence was as useful as possible, she turned her horse around and headed back towards her manor house.

Seated at the large oaken worktable in the manor's library, Beatrix took quill and parchment. She outlined the rumour and detailed the meeting with Isabel. When she finished the writing, she dusted fine sand on it to prevent it from smearing, folded the parchment and sealed it with wax from a candle on the table. She impressed her signet ring containing the family crest onto the warm, soft wax and summoned her footman.

"Samuel, take this message to undersheriff Alric. It has important information regarding the murder of Thomas the lecturer. so please deliver it at once."

"Aye, my lady. I will summon the groom to prepare my horse, and I shall leave immediately."

He left in haste, and soon knocked on the undersheriff's door.

"Well, Samuel, to what do I owe the honour of a visit from my lady's footman?" Alric was puzzled, but he held a welcoming expression and spoke in a pleasant tone.

"I have an important message from my lady Beatrix, Master Alric, and she begs you read it at your earliest convenience."

"And so, I shall. Thank your mistress for sending it to me. I assume it concerns the murder of young Thomas?"

"Indeed, it does, Master. She was clear about its importance in that regard."

"Very well, Samuel. You may tell your mistress that I will attend to this directly. And thank her for sending it, please."

"Aye, Master. And now I must be off for the manor house. I shall deliver your message."

After Samuel left, the undersheriff broke the waxen seal and read the finely written, elegant script. As he read, his eyes squinted with concern. "This may or may not be true," he mused, "but I have heard no such rumours. I am suspicious."

Calling a constable to come and bring his horse, Alric planned to go where rumours may most easily be found: *The Black Swan Tavern.*

Brother Ambrose – Another Suspect

Brother Ambrose meditated in the abbey's chapel. The loss of his friend, Thomas, was a heavy burden. As he knelt at a prie-dieu, he felt a presence behind him. He started to rise.

"Do not rise, brother," a voice whispered. "I must tell someone, but I do not know who to tell. I have a heavy burden, but it must remain a secret."

Ambrose was puzzled. The voice whispered so quietly that he could not discover just who it was. "But I am not your confessor," Ambrose responded. "You should take this to your confessor."

"I cannot, brother. I need practical advice. The time to cleanse my soul will come later, but now I must beg your advice."

"Very well. Speak your concerns and I will try to help you. But mark you, I cannot offer forgiveness. That must be the role of the confessor. However, I can offer secrecy if that is any comfort to you."

"That is kind of you, Brother, but I must not hold you to that. Attend my tale and you will see why." The lay brother's voice was becoming slightly louder as concern began overtook him.

"I was at the abbey gate when Gilbert the Bladesmith departed after sharpening the abbey's knives. I saw him go in the direction of a fire at the abbey wall. I did not follow him. I am sure now that Gilbert the Bladesmith killed the lecturer. I could have stopped him, but I did not. I am responsible for the lecturer's death."

Ambrose listened to the voice carefully. He became increasingly certain that it was the voice of Wulfric, a newly accepted lay brother.

"Brother, this should be reported to the undersheriff. However, I need not identify you. And, yes, I recognize your voice Brother Wulfric." When Wulfric spoke, it was in a low, rasping, whisper.

"Aye, 'tis I. You are correct. Tell the undersheriff if you must but please protect my name. I will confess my sin, of course, but I swear, I did not intend to shirk my duty so."

"I am sure that you didn't Wulfric and, in truth, you are not responsible for the lecturer's death. But your story is important, and it must go before the undersheriff."

"Very well, if you must. But if 'tis possible, please do not betray me."

"I shan't if there be any way to prevent it."

Undersheriff Alric the Bald looked at the carefully written message delivered to him from Rewley Abbey. "Hmmm," he thought, "now we have gone from no suspects to two. And, maybe, three."

# CHAPTER 15: A SILENT PLEDGE

In which we visit Another Autopsy and Sister Agnes's deepening resolve to unveil the truth.

Undersheriff Alric knocked upon the door of Gilbert's room at the college. Irritated at the interruption to his studies, Gilbert stomped to the door, grumbling. "Who is it? I'm busy. Go away."

"It's Undersheriff Alric, boy. Open the door," the voice commanded.

Irritated at the interruption, Gilbert opened the door. The undersheriff strode into the cramped space, a scowl darkening his features.

"What now, Undersheriff? What is this about, then? That tavern wench, Mateld, again? Are you still going on about that slut's accusations?" Gilbert's voice was laced with annoyance and contempt.

"Nay, Master Gilbert. 'Tis far more grave than tavern squabbles. Your father has been found robbed and murdered in his butcher's shop. You must come with me," Alric announced, his tone sombre, yet urgent.

Gilbert – The Butcher Shop

Gilbert paled at the undersheriff's words. "No, that is not possible. I saw him just two days ago."

"Master Gilbert, I am afraid that it is possible, and, in fact, such is the case. Now, come with me, please." It was not a request as much as it was an order. Tears running down his cheeks, Gilbert followed the Undersheriff out the door of his room.

The undersheriff had a cart waiting. Gilbert ascended to the empty seat and was joined by the undersheriff. "I want to get us to your father's shop as quickly as possible, Master Gilbert. It is important that you identify your father, even though everyone in Oxford town knows him. Just a formality, you understand."

"Of course, Sheriff. It is just that this was quite unexpected, and I confess that I am finding it difficult."

"I understand, Master Gilbert, but, even in difficult times we all do what we must." And they arrived at the butcher shop.

Gilbert's father was covered with a large rug when they walked up to his body. "There's no blood," thought Gilbert. "I wonder why?"

The undersheriff pulled the rug back from the dead man's head, exposing his face. "Can you identify this man, Master Gilbert?"

"Yes. Of course. It is my father. Now can you please take me out of here and back to the college?"

"Gilbert clearly is irritated at something," thought the undersheriff. "I wonder what has him so on edge. He just has seen his murdered father's body." And the undersheriff filed that thought away for future consideration.

"Thank you, Master Gilbert. Just a formality. I am sure that you understand." Not a question but a statement of fact. The undersheriff called to one of his constables, "Take this man back to Baliol and his room, William, and then return here immediately."

"Aye, sir." And the constable escorted Gilbert to the cart in which the undersheriff brought him to the butcher shop.

Undersheriff Alric turned back towards the corpse. He

examined it without moving it or touching it. "There be something not right here. Constable John…"

"Aye, sir?" The constable left his post at the door of the butcher shop and walked quickly over to the Undersheriff.

"You must do this quickly, for the day passes. Do you know where Aylesbridge manor is?"

"Aye, sir. I have been there before."

"Get a cart and the fastest horse you can find, go there and fetch Lady Beatrix here at once. It is urgent."

"Aye sir, on my way."

"Constable Edward… see to it that nobody enters the shop or touches Master Edmund's body until the Lady arrives."

"Aye sir. I will just stay here between the door and Master Edmund's body."

Lady Beatrix – The Crime Scene

Lady Beatrix was in the garden of the manor house trimming roses to decorate her chamber. While her lady's maid usually did this task, today Beatrix felt like enjoying the warm breezes and fragrances from her garden. She was lost in thought as she selected the best rich, red blooms – not too young to show their beauty, and not too old that they may die before making their impression on her chamber's visitors. They would go into her outer chamber, the sitting room, of course. Nobody but her personal maid Margery ever entered her bed chamber.

Margery aroused Beatrix abruptly from her reverie. "My lady, there is a constable inside insisting that you come with him at once. He says that 'tis most urgent."

"Whatever can he want?" Beatrix mused as she

gathered up the delicate rose cuttings and followed Margery. "Well, let us see what he's about. Ask Samuel to join us."

"Very well, my lady. The constable is in the library awaiting you."

Lady Beatrix handed the roses to one of the parlour maids, "Put these in my sitting room and arrange them to brighten up the room," and she was off for the library.

As she entered the room, the constable turned to her. By the look on his face, it was clear to Beatrix that this was a visit of utmost urgency. She also noted that he seemed nervous at being in her presence.

"How may I help you, Constable?"

"I am called Constable John," he stammered. "Undersheriff Alric requests that you join him at the butcher shop on the high street. There has been a murder, and he begs that you examine the body. I have a cart for you."

"No cart is required, John. I shall ride. It is much faster. Samuel, have my groom prepare my fastest horse. I shall attend him when I have changed into more suitable attire. John, I certainly will arrive at the butcher shop before you so I shall explain to the undersheriff that it was my requirement and no fault of yours," and she headed for the sweeping staircase and her rooms.

Lady Beatrix arrived shortly at the butcher shop. A constable took her horse as she dismounted and walked it to the rear of the shop where it might have water and some grain after its hard run.

"Good day to you, Master Alric. Your constable was quite insistent that your request was urgent, so I decided to dismiss him and his cart and ride here on my fastest horse. So, how may I help you today? I see that you have a murder scene here but beyond that I know nothing."

"Thank you for coming my lady. The owner of this shop was Master Edmund of Shrewsbury, a well-known and well-regarded merchant. It is clear that there has been a robbery. I did not ask Master Gilbert about that part of the crime, when he identified his father's body, because he likely would not know. However, he identified his father, right enough. If I may beg your indulgence, would you please look the body over. I know that this may not be a proper request for a lady, but I know that you and Sister Agnes examined the body of Thomas the Lecturer."

"There is no problem, Undersheriff. Please remove the covering, and I just will have a look."

As soon as the rug was removed, exposing the corpse, Beatrix took an abrupt step back. "I must go immediately to the Abbey, Undersheriff. Sister Agnes must see this. She is far more able than I to examine such a violent death. And, unless I am much mistaken, she will want to examine the body in great detail. There are contradictions, you see, but I must let her expound upon that. Have your constable bring my horse at once please. The day grows late, and I expect that you will need to get the body to the abbey at once."

Lady Beatrix and Sister Agnes – The Abbey

Escorted to Sister Agnes' workroom by the Mother Superior, Beatrix, breathless after her hard ride, short though it may have been, confronted Agnes.

"A very good day to you, Sister. I come with an urgent request from the undersheriff."

"From the undersheriff, is it? Well, it must be of quite some import for him to make a request of a humble servant of the Lord. Pray, what is it that he wants of us?"

"He has another murder, Sister. This one is strange. I'll let you discover that for yourself if you agree to look at the body."

Mother Alice interrupted. "What is it that you believe only Sister Agnes can add to the undersheriff's investigation, Lady Beatrix?"

"This is no simple murder, Mother. The man's throat has been slit the width of his neck, yet there is no blood at the scene. He appears to have died where he was attacked and fell but the absence of blood puzzles me greatly."

"Very well. Sister Agnes, if you wish to pursue this, in light of our previous conversation with the undersheriff, you may do so. But keep your usual detailed notes of your procedures and findings and ensure that I receive a copy."

"Certainly, Mother. I shall do all that you ask." Turning to Beatrix, "You should return to the undersheriff, my lady and tell him to come with all speed. My novice will await you and the cart at the servant's gate. I will prepare my work room. But before he puts Edmund's form in a cart, please look it over closely so that you can answer any questions that I might have regarding the scene and Master Edmund's form. And do not let his form out of your sight until the undersheriff arrives here with it."

"That I will, Sister." She headed for the gate of the abbey, a stable boy brought her horse, and she was away to town.

It was just after Vespers, and shortly before dusk that Beatrix, the undersheriff and the cart containing Edmund's body arrived at the back gate of the abbey. As promised, the novice Isabel was waiting at the gate.

The undersheriff greeted sister Agnes with a concerned look. "Lady Beatrix seems greatly concerned by something she saw when she first examined the body, Sister. You know that we must proceed quickly, but with caution. The deputy coroner will certainly want to perform an inquest and your results could be quite important."

"I will do what I may, Undersheriff, but I cannot anticipate results before I examine Master Edmund's form completely. Then, I will gladly convey all that I observe through Lady Beatrix for the inquest."

"You know that inquests should be held as soon as possible after the discovery of the crime, Sister..." the undersheriff seemed nervous.

"Fear not Master Alric. We will complete our work as rapidly as may be without sacrificing our results."

"Thank you, Sister. I am glad that you grasp the urgency of this procedure. Now I must return to my inquiries."

"Also, please leave two of your constables to observe and assist with moving Master Edmund's form when necessary. God go with you, Undersheriff." "And with you, Sister. Two of my men shall remain here with you."

Sister Agnes called for her novice, "Isabel, please come into my workroom and bring your writing instruments along with some parchment. I will need detailed notes for Mother when we complete this task."

"Certainly, Sister. I will be there anon."

Sister Agnes left the workroom and went to the chapel to pray for wisdom in her undertaking. She also prayed for the soul of Master Edmund. When she returned to her workroom, Edmund's body was laid out on her worktable covered with a cloth. Agnes pulled back the cloth, revealing most of Edmund's form.

"Is this exactly how you found him my lady?"

"Indeed 'tis, sister. I asked the undersheriff as well and

he told me that the body had not been moved since he and his men were called to the butcher shop."

Lady Beatrix noted Agnes' use of the term "form" instead of "body." She assumed that the nun was considering the church position that the soul and the body were separate and, while the body – or, form – died, the soul ascended to heaven. She made a mental note to respect the dignity of the appellation and use it herself in the future when speaking with Sister Agnes or her sister nuns.

The novice, Isabel, entered the workroom with her portable writing desk. She put it on a small worktable at the head of Agnes' larger one, being careful not to get too close. The scents of candles and purifying herbs in the room could become overpowering and Isabel feared that she would faint from the odors in the room and the smell of death if she got too close to the form of Edmund lying on the table.

She opened her writing desk revealing its several ink pots, quill pens, small sharp knives for sharpening her quills and some sheets of parchment. She took one of the parchment sheets, placed it on the sloped writing surface built into the desk, sharpened a quill, and opened an ink pot. She was ready to begin her notetaking.

Agnes paused briefly to offer a prayer for wisdom to Saint Hildegard, a 12th century Benedictine abbess, Saint Benedict, Saint Luke the Evangelist, patron saint of healers, and the Virgin Mary referring to her as *Sedes Sapientiae* or *Seat of Wisdom*. She offered another brief prayer for the soul of Edmund and began her task.

Sister Agnes and Lady Beatrix – Another Autopsy

Agnes walked around the body, making close inspection of the knife wounds and the brutal slash across the throat. She stepped over to her smaller writing desk and from the shelf above it fetched her magnifying stone. Although they were several feet from the worktable and Edmund's body, the constables showed rapt attention to the proceedings. One of them spoke up, "Sister, what is that thing in your hand? I never have seen such in all my years. It makes small things look large."

"It is called a magnifying stone, Constable. With it I can observe details that I might otherwise miss."

"'Tis uncanny how it makes those wounds appear so big."

Bending over the wound to Edmund's throat, Agnes moved the stone across it observing very closely. She was particularly interested in the ends of the wound.

"This wound is from left to right as Master Edmund's form is lying. If the wound was inflicted with Edmund's form as it is now, the killer would needs be left-handed. If, however, Master Edmund was standing and his attacker came from behind, the killer was right-handed."

She summoned Beatrix. "My lady, I would demonstrate the application of the knife to the victim if approached from the rear. With all respect, Lady Beatrix, would you consent to playing the role of the victim and I the killer?"

Beatrix thought for a moment "How will this demonstration compromise me in sight of these constables and the novice? No matter. It must be done." To Agnes, "Sister, you know that you may depend upon me. I trust your intentions. It is critically important that we determine the true nature of the wound to the throat. Further, we have not yet determined why there is no blood at the wound. If we may work out these important points, I gladly would put my trust in your care and wisdom. You may proceed, Sister. Constables, you may be assured that I will come to no harm during this demonstration."

"Your trust and willingness to help solve this heinous crime are gratifying, my lady." She turned to the constables. "You may wait without. I shall summon you when we are finished with this demonstration." Turning to Isabel, "Isabel, you will record in detail all that you observe and read it back to me when I request. Mind your Latin. The description must be as clear as possible."

The room was still and the air heavy as the two constables departed. Beatrix stood in front of Agnes with her back to the nun. The only sound in the workroom was the scratching of Isabel's quill upon her parchment. Agnes picked up one of Isabel's quills.

"My lady, rather than demonstrate this using a knife, with your permission I shall use this quill in its place."

"As you wish, Sister."

"First, I will place the quill in my left hand. This is an almost impossible position." Drawing the quill across Beatrix's throat, Agnes observed, "I am the same height as you, my lady. So, you can observe that the stroke is straight and even with the exception that the position is so awkward that completing a smooth cut is nearly impossible. If I were taller, one end would be higher than the other and if I were shorter, the other end would be higher. But the cut is straight. Shall we infer that the killer is the same height as Master Edmund? I think not. It would not be possible for the cut to be so smooth if the killer, regardless of height, tried to attack left-handed."

She shifted the quill to her right hand. "Now I will make the same demonstration with the quill in my right hand. Look, you… the cut is straight, and the position of the killer is comfortable, unlike when we used the left hand. Now, recall that I said that the cut is from left to right. I know that because the depth of the cut is greater on the left end.

So, may we assume that the killer came from behind and attacked Master Edmund from left to right with the knife in his right hand and that the killer is about the same height as the victim? Not yet. We still do not know why there is no blood in this wound.

Isabel, you my finish your notes on this demonstration and then summon the constables. They may return and observe that there is no harm to Lady Beatrix. And to you my lady, I am grateful for your assistance. We now have a clearer picture though, by no means, do we have a solution to the crime."

Isabel left the workroom and returned with the constables. "Constables, thank you for your cooperation. You will note that no harm has come to our distinguished guest."

Agnes returned to her worktable and retrieved her magnifying stone. She walked around the body several times, observing the depth and angle of the many knife wounds.

"There is nothing of interest here, my lady. These puncture wounds all are superficial, and they show only that he who inflicted the wounds, with the exception of the throat, was standing above Master Edmund. The throat wound is an unanswered question. Certainly, if the throat wound was the cause of death, the puncture wounds would not have bled. But we have no blood at the throat, and there is no indication that his form has been cleansed. Further, that wound would have bled profusely soaking his robe and apron as we saw in the murder of Master Thomas. Such is not the case." She turned to the constables. "Please turn over the form of Master Edmund.

The two constables moved to the worktable and, respectfully, using the cover to turn him over repositioned him on the table. As Sister Agnes folded back the cover from over his head, she stepped back with a gasp of surprise.

"God's bones!" exclaimed the constable nearest Edmund's head. Immediately he crossed himself, "Oh! I'm sorry, sister, my lady. I was shocked at the sight of his head. I've seen such a wound before."

Isabel, standing at her writing desk at the head of the worktable, felt her knees grow weak. As she started to sink to the floor, Sister Agnes and Lady Beatrix intercepted her and lowered her gently into her chair.

"Constable, please get the water jug from my table by the window and bring the cup beside it."

"Aye, sister, at once." The water brought, Sister Agnes dampened a cloth and gently wiped Isabel's face.

"Sister – what happened? Oh! That wound! I never have seen such."

"Here, Isabel. Take some water. Constable," speaking to the other constable, "when she is able, please take Sister Isabel out into the fresh air for a moment. When she feels better, please bring her back. I know that this is difficult, Sister, but you must persevere. We will need a detailed drawing of this wound as part of your notes."

"Certainly, Sister. It is just that the wound is so horrible to look upon," and Isabel left slowly with the constable.

Turning to the constable remaining in the room, Agnes asked, "Constable, you said you have seen this type of wound before?"

"Aye, Sister. It were in battle and a war horse kicked a man in the back of his head. Killed 'im at once, it did." The constable bent down to get a closer look and started to lift a long shard of wood from the wound.

"No! Do not touch the wound, Constable, until Isabel can draw it for our records."

"Sorry, again, Sister," the constable was becoming embarrassed at his repeated violations of protocol.

Agnes fetched her magnifying stone from Isabel's table where she had set it earlier. Bending down over the wound, she examined the long wooden shard as well as the wound in which it was embedded.

She thought to herself for a moment, "My lady Beatrix, through her gift of copies of Master Galen's studies, is giving us the knowledge to observe and draw conclusions about this injury. They will be the key to enlarging upon the source and results of Master Edmund's injuries." She turned to Lady Beatrix,

"Master Galen, authority on the human form, speaking to us from the distant past through your generous gift of his manuscripts, writes of the balance of the veins and nerves at the base of the skull. His writings suggest that a severe injury to this area, such as the one we observe in Master Edmund, could be fatal. It would stop the heart's pumping blood to the rest of his form instantly. Constable, your observation regarding the similar wound you witnessed echoes Galen's teachings."

Isabel entered the room with the constable, looking at her solicitously, fearing that she may again faint as she approached Edmund's body. However, Isabel, mindful of her duty walked purposefully to her writing desk. "I am ready Sister."

"Isabel, before you begin taking notes of our

observations, please use my magnifying stone to draw the wound. Be as accurate and detailed as you can. Be sure not to miss the long wooden shard penetrating the wound itself. Are you ready to do that?"

"Of course, sister. I simply was overcome for a moment. It is warm in here and the herbs and candles make the air thick and heavy. Let us proceed," and she picked up the magnifying stone, examining the wound closely and drawing the wound one line at a time, using assorted colours to highlight the various nerves and veins as Agnes pointed them out to her.

Once Isabel had completed her drawing, Agnes commenced her dictation for Isabel's notes. But, before she did so, she took a long, pointed pair of tweezers from the work tools on her shelf and carefully teased the long shard of wood from the wound. She took out the silken cloth in which she was collecting pieces of evidence from the first murder and added the shard to her collection.

Lady Beatrix, meanwhile, had approached the body of Edmund and was examining the wound carefully. Seeming to see something of interest she reached over the body to fetch Agnes' magnifying stone. Moving down his right shoulder from the wound, she observed a faint blue and violet bruise, almost hidden by the growth of hair on Edmund's shoulders.

"Look you, Sister. The attacker was right-handed, it would appear."

Agnes took the stone and examined the bruise carefully. "Perhaps, my lady, perhaps. Let us look more closely." Agnes walked around the table to observe the left shoulder. Seeing nothing unusual, she walked back towards where she had been standing, halting abruptly as she passed Edmund's right leg.

"We cannot say with certainty, my lady, but look you at the bruise by Edmund's knee. This suggests that he was knocked to his knees before the fatal blow was struck. The bruise on his shoulder suggests that he was hit, but not as hard as the fatal blow that knocked him down. This initial blow could be from either a right- or left-handed man.

Avicenna's Canon, also generously provided by you, my lady, as well as Master Galen's works suggest that the two bruises were administered prior to death and would likely have resulted in or from a fall to his knees by Master Edmund. I believe that the wound to Master Edmund's throat will help us determine in which hand the attacker held his weapon.

One more thing. See the colour of his back. It is a dark purplish color."

Agnes selected a small sharp-pointed probe from her tool shelf on the wall near the worktable. She carefully pressed the point into the discolored area of Master Edmund's back. Immediately a dark-coloured liquid oozed from the puncture wound. "Look you, my lady. This is blood, partially congealed and starting to putrefy.

Galen and Avicenna tell us that the body's humours and vital fluids respond to trauma and illness in ways which we can observe. Careful examination of these responses can help us understand the underlying cause of Master Edmund's death. Master Edmund's circulatory system and injuries help us to interpret what we see. See how the blood has settled in his back. That can help us understand how and when these injuries were inflicted.

Liquids, such as blood and other humours flow to the lowest part of the victim's form if his heart was not beating. This suggests that he was placed on his back after death. The bruises and the damage to his skull would have forced his form to fall forward. But he was found lying on his back. Is that not so, Constable?"

"Aye, Sister. That were how we found 'im."

"Isabel, please make certain that your notes reflect our discoveries, Lady Beatrix's discovery of the bruises and the conclusions we draw from them as well as my question to the constable and his answer."

"Yes, Sister. I have it all."

"Now, constables, please turn Master Edmund over and place him on the floor exactly as you found him at the butcher shop. Treat his form gently and with respect."

The two constables gently picked up the body and placed it on the floor carefully turning it onto his back. They stepped aside as sister Agnes picked up Isabel's quill as she had done while demonstrating on Lady Beatrix. Walking slowly and carefully she stood astride the body facing his head.

"Now, my lady, would you please remove the covering from his face so that I can see the neck wound?" Reaching down, Sister Agnes with the feather in her right hand, made a cutting motion across Edmund's throat, moving from the body's left to its right. "As you see, my lady, it is quite awkward to stand this way and, with the quill in my right hand, cut across from Master Edmund's left to his right. It would be more natural to cut from right to left, but by examination of the wound with the magnifying stone we see that the wound was introduced from left to right."

Taking the quill in her left hand, Agnes made a cutting motion across Edmund's neck from his left to his right.

"Notice that this position and the cutting motion is natural for the attacker. So, my lady, we may conclude that the attacker was left-handed. When he struck the fatal blow, the attacker must have been somewhat to the right of

Master Edmund. We also may conclude that the attacker likely was somewhat shorter, but not by very much, than Master Edmund because he knocked Master Edmund to his knees before delivering the fatal blow. The wound across his throat did not bleed as did not the punctures because Master Edmund's heart had stopped pumping blood. Constables, you may gently return Master Edmund's form to the worktable. Place him on his back."

On the worktable pulling down the cover down to expose the puncture wounds, Sister Agnes took her small probe and carefully measured the depth of each puncture would. "These wounds are quite shallow, my lady. I believe they were the product of the attacker's rage, now mostly spent after his other exertions. Also, see the angle of my probe. All the puncture wounds slant slightly upwards. That is what we might expect if the attacker was astride Master Edmund's form when he made the punctures."

One of the constables looked puzzled. "Beggin' yer pardon, my lady, but how does a high-born lady of wealth and position come to be muckin' about with murder?"

"Quite simple, Constable," Beatrix was slightly annoyed at the constable's question. Her status as a lady from a noble family was none of his business. However, thinking for a moment, "my family are benefactors of this convent and, especially this infirmary and Sister Agnes. I have had plenty of opportunity to observe the fruits of our sustenance firsthand, as you see today."

As Beatrix was addressing the constable, Mother Alice, the mother superior, entered the workroom. Isabel was just finishing her notes and stepped back away from the worktable.

"Well, Sister Agnes, what say you? Have you learned anything yet?"

"Indeed, we have, Mother. We know that Master Edmund's murder was born out of rage. We know that the killer is left-handed. And we know that he died from a blow to his skull with a heavy club or a mallet. Finally, we know that he was moved from a position of lying face down to lying upon his back after the murder and that the killer was slightly shorter than Master Edmund."

"Very good, Sister. Please make sure that I have a copy of your notes, so that if I am asked, I will have full and complete answers. Now, may we turn Master Edmund over to the undersheriff?"

"We may, Mother. And I will have a copy of Isabel's notes for him as well."

"It strikes me, Sister, that they are aspects of this murder that are remarkably similar to the killing of Master Thomas."

"I had thought of that, Mother. I have preserved a piece of evidence that may help tie the two together. No doubt the undersheriff will make a similar observation."

No sooner had the exchange between Sister Agnes and the mother superior ended than a novice requested entry to the workroom. She was escorting Undersheriff Alric the Bald.

The abbess turned to the novice, "Please escort Undersheriff Alric in, sister. Master Alric, a very good day to you. I assume that you are here to take possession of Master Edmund?"

"I am, indeed, Mother. And have you learned anything about the murder from your examinations, Sister?

"Indeed, we certainly have, Master Alric" and Agnes described their findings in detail as she had for Mother Alice, leaving out mention of the wooden shard.

"This is impressive work, Sister, and Lady Beatrix. Will

I have the notes from this to take to the inquest? The deputy coroner can be quite demanding, you know."

"Undersheriff, Lady Beatrix, who has been in here with me the entire time that I took to complete the examination, will be present at the inquest to report on our findings here. In fact, she participated in drawing our conclusions."

"That will suffice, Sister. Of course, I understand that it would not be right for you to attend in person, but I am sure with your notes and Lady Beatrix, we will accomplish that which we intend to." And, after placing the body on a stretcher, the constables and the undersheriff departed the abbey.

"God go with you, Undersheriff."

"And with you as well, Mother."

Lady Beatrix – The Coroner's Inquest and a Surprise

"Place the shard and our other evidence in your girdle pouch, my lady. Be certain that they are not lost or misplaced."

"Of course, Sister. My pouch never leaves my belt when I am out of the manor house." Beatrix opened her delicately embroidered girdle pouch, took the items wrapped in fine linen from Agnes and placed them inside. She then tied the pouch's cord, ensuring that the items of evidence would stay safe. "I will take my carriage to the castle where the Inquest is to be held. I also have copies of Isabel's notes in my pouch for the undersheriff and the deputy coroner." And Beatrix left, meeting her carriage outside the abbey's main gate.

When Beatrix arrived at the castle, Adam de

Wallingford, deputy coroner was on hand to meet her as they disembarked from her carriage. Bowing slightly, he said, "We are honoured by your presence, my lady, but why, exactly, are you here at this grisly affair? This hardly is the place for a lady of substance such as yourself to visit."

"Good afternoon, Master Deputy Coroner. I am here representing Sister Agnes who, for obvious reasons may not attend a gathering of this sort."

"Very well, my lady. Please allow me to escort you to the great hall where we will assemble to determine the manner and cause of Master Edmund's death. I'm certain that there will be much that you can tell us."

When they had arrived in the great hall, Beatrix noted some of the others who were in attendance. She particularly noted the undersheriff and his two constables. The deputy coroner seated her at his immediate right hand with his scribe on his immediate left. Servants entered the hall with mugs of ale and mead for the jury and witnesses and the deputy coroner called the inquest to order. The transcript of the inquest as taken down by the scribe is as follows:

Deputy Coroner Adam de Wallingford: *"I am calling this inquest to order. Master scribe, you may begin your notes." His voice, deep and authoritative, echoed through the large, high-ceilinged hall with its stone walls, family shields, and tapestries, present not for decoration alone, but to allow the room, heated by two huge fireplaces, to remain warm in winter.*

However, Beatrix, observing closely, noted that the deputy coroner seemed uncomfortable, perhaps at her presence. She would fix that in her testimony.

Deputy Coroner Adam de Wallingford: *"I call*

Undersheriff Alric the Bald to testify. Undersheriff, when you arrived at the scene of the murder, what did you observe?"

Undersheriff Alric the Bald*: "The shop's proprietor, Master Edmund was lying on his back dead. Nearby I found this large mallet, used for dispatching cattle. I suspect this was the murder weapon, but I cannot say because the blood on it could be from a human or from cattle."*

Deputy Coroner Adam de Wallingford: *"And did you or your men observe anything else, Undersheriff?"*

Undersheriff Alric the Bald*: "Yes. The iron box that contained the shop's money was empty with the lock broken."*

Deputy Coroner Adam de Wallingford: *"And that was all?"*

Undersheriff Alric the Bald*: "Yes, master deputy coroner."*

Deputy Coroner Adam de Wallingford*: "Constables... do you have anything to add? Let the record show that the two constables have indicated "no" as their answer."*

Deputy Coroner Adam de Wallingford*: "Lady Beatrix, would you like to give your testimony now?"*

Lady Beatrix: *"Yes, but I entreat that we adjourn to the place where the deceased is kept. Since my testimony has to do with postmortem observations, it may be easier for the jury if I could point out the findings in situ."*

One of the jurors: *"Master Deputy Coroner... most unseemly. Women of Lady Beatrix's rank should not be permitted, let alone requested to be around the body. It is beneath her."*

Deputy Coroner Adam de Wallingford*: "In fact, Sir*

Henry it is necessary. Lady Beatrix assisted at the postmortem examination of the body and is the only one here suited to relate her, and Sister Agnes' findings in this court. Sister Agnes herself performed the postmortem examination with Lady Beatrix beside her. Master Undersheriff, do you agree?"

Undersheriff Alric the Bald*: "Yes, Master. I certainly do. Lady Beatrix was present, participated alongside Sister Agnes and is the right person to convey their findings to us."*

Deputy Coroner Adam de Wallingford*: "Then we shall proceed to the body."*

Sir Henry: *"I still do not like it. It is most unbecoming for a lady of her esteemed station to soil her hands with the dealings of the deceased."*

Deputy Coroner Adam de Wallingford*: "Your chivalry is noted, Sir Henry but we will proceed to collect all of the facts such that justice may be done."*

Within a few moments the Deputy Coroner's retinue had gathered around the worktable holding Edmund's earthly remains. The constables carefully and respectfully removed the cover from over the body and Lady Beatrix began.

Lady Beatrix: *"Gentlemen of this esteemed jury, I bid you direct your attention to the grievous wound located at the base of Master Edmund's skull. Constables will you turn him over, please?"*

As the constables complied, Lady Beatrix continued.

Lady Beatrix: *"Note the large wound at the base of Edmund's skull. We probed the wound and it extends to Edmund's brain itself. Authorities on the human body tell us that this blow was enough to extinguish Master Edmund's life. Master Undersheriff, will you please fetch the heavy mallet that you believe might have been the* *murder weapon?"*

The undersheriff complied, returning quickly with the large, blood-covered mallet.

Lady Beatrix: *"Now Undersheriff, you say that we cannot distinguish human blood from animal blood on this mallet. Correct?"*

Undersheriff Alric the Bald*: "Indeed, my lady. That is as I believe it to be."*

Lady Beatrix: *"You are correct, Master Undersheriff. So, we must have another method to place this mallet in the hands of the killer." Lady Beatrix was savoring the drama caused by her short pause and her words sunk in.*

Lady Beatrix: *Now I am removing a piece of important evidence from my girdle pouch. Note you all that this is a shard of wood, containing blood. Do you recall this, Master Undersheriff? Constables?"*

Deputy Coroner Adam de Wallingford*: "Let your notes indicate that all three responded affirmatively, Master Scribe."*

Lady Beatrix: *"Now, master Undersheriff, please bring you the mallet that we may examine it more closely."*

Lady Beatrix carefully slid the shard into a groove on the mallet where, clearly, it had broken off.

Lady Beatrix: *As you can see, gentlemen of the jury, the shard fits perfectly, even to the patterns of blood on both the shard and the mallet. This is the murder weapon."*

There were audible gasps from the jury members.

Deputy Coroner Adam de Wallingford*: "It is quite clear my lady that you and Sister Agnes have uncovered the murder weapon, but the body was found on its back. How can that be?"*

Lady Beatrix: *"Look you at the two small bruises, one* *on his shoulder and one on his knee. These indicate that Master Edmund was struck from behind on his shoulder which caused him to fall to his knees. Then, the killer delivered the fatal blow to his head. Afterwords, the killer turned the body over so that it was lying on his back. We know that the blood in the body, because the heart was not beating to circulate the blood, pooled in his back where Sister Agnes was able to withdraw some partially clotted blood that was beginning to putrefy as has been observed in the infirmary, and supported by the esteemed writings of Galen and Avicenna, and as the nature of Master Edmund's wounds suggests. After the killer turned Master Edmund's body over, he slashed the throat and made the numerous puncture wounds in the chest."*

Deputy Coroner Adam de Wallingford: *"If that is so, my lady, why did not these wounds bleed?"*

Lady Beatrix: "*According to the teachings of Galen and Avicenna, the grave injury to Master Edmund disrupted his vital forces. Without the heart's motion and the flow of vital spirit, his blood ceased to move, which is why the wounds inflicted upon him after his death did not bleed."*

Deputy Coroner Adam de Wallingford: *"What else have you to report, my lady?"*

Lady Beatrix: *We know that the attacker was left-handed. The explanation for that conclusion appears in our notes, of which you and the jury have copies. The numerous stab wounds suggest rage against the victim. We also know that the killer is slightly shorter than Master Edmund. The explanation for that also is in our notes."*

Deputy Coroner Adam de Wallingford: *"Gentlemen of the jury, have you questions for this witness?"*

Sir Henry: *"No, Master, we do not. But after discussing* *this testimony among ourselves, we are ready to give the verdict."*

Deputy Coroner Adam de Wallingford*: "Very well, Sir Henry. What say you and what say you all?"*

Sir Henry: *"Master Deputy Coroner, we, the jury in this inquest into the death of Master Edmund, find that the manner of death was murder by person, or persons not currently known, and that the cause of death was the blow to Master Edmund's head. So say we all."*

Deputy Coroner Adam de Wallingford*: "Very well Sir Henry. Master Scribe, see that the jury's verdict and the testimony of the witnesses are laid down in your writings and prepare them for my signature. I adjourn this inquiry."*

The sun was beginning to set, the skies growing grey with the lateness of the day. The undersheriff approached Lady Beatrix as the jury and the deputy coroner were departing. "My lady, your testimony was valuable. We now know that the killer likely is left-handed, slightly shorter than Master Edmund, and given to uncontrollable rage."

"That is correct Master Undersheriff. Now I must return to the abbey. Sister Agnes certainly will want to hear the results of this inquest."

"Of course. I must admit, your conclusions, your use of accepted teachings and the experience and knowledge of Sister Agnes were important in finding this heinous murderer. Do you believe that the same killer was responsible for the murder of Thomas?"

"I will need to defer to Sister Agnes for that answer, Master Undersheriff. But, speaking for myself only, I would not be surprised to find it so."

"Thank you, my lady. May I have one of my constables escort you to the Abbey? It is starting to get a bit late in the day."

"I appreciate the offer, Master, but the abbey is not far. I will speak with Sister Agnes and then we shall attend vespers and share a meal with the other nuns. I shall spend the night in the abbey. My coachman will return to the manor house and come for me in the morning."

"Very well, my lady. Please offer my thanks to Sister Agnes. God go with you." "And with you Master Undersheriff." Beatrix stepped into her coach and was gone.

Beatrix and Sister Agnes – The Inquest

Beatrix's coachman drove up to the gates of Godstow Abbey, dismounted from the carriage and pounded at the large door. The gate was a formidable entrance, soaring above the visitors' heads, clad with strong iron straps, and hung on massive hinges. Its purpose, protecting the abbey's community from outside encroachment and acting as a symbolic boundary between the secular and spiritual world was obvious. Set in the centre of the gate was a large cross, carved into the wood of the massive door.

A novice opened the gate and, recognizing Beatrix, took her directly to Agnes' workroom. "Welcome, my lady. How went the inquest?"

"It went very well, Sister. The only question I could not answer was from the undersheriff: 'Was this the same killer who dispatched Thomas.' I suggested he speak with you for certainty."

"And rightly so, my lady. Of course, as we suspect the same hand behind these acts, justice now appears clearer for the undersheriff. His inquiry progresses.

Now, shall we turn our thoughts to prayer and reflection at Vespers, and afterward, the companionship of the evening meal?"

"Yes, Sister, I would appreciate that." And the two ladies – a cloistered nun, in her middle years but still handsome with the wrinkles of age barely visible, and a noblewoman of high birth, glowing with youth belying her five and twenty years – departed the workroom as if they were, in truth, sisters.

CHAPTER 16: TAVERN TALES

In which the gathering information from the local tavern unveils the underbelly of Oxford and the undersheriff receives a message from beyond.

The undersheriff and his two deputies sat in the Black Swan Inn. Mateld brought tankards of ale and wandered slowly back to the bar hoping to hear some gossip about the latest murder: the butcher shop keeper. But the lawmen kept their silence until she was well out of earshot.

"We really must get this under control. The town will come apart, everyone blaming everyone else."

"Master Alric, I don't know what we can do except continuing to look."

"You are probably right Constable, but we must keep trying. Is there any news among the townspeople? Does anyone know anything that can get us started?"

"Not a whisper, Master Alric."

"Well finish your ale and go out and keep digging. Somebody knows something."

"I've heard tell ye're the undersheriff 'round these parts of the Shire. I've a song upon me lips that ye'll be keen to hear, for it holds the key to unraveling a mystery most foul."

Alexis, Bard of the Shire
– A Proposition for the Undersheriff

"And who might you be, Mistress?"

"Alexis, Bard of the Shire, I am. Me kin and I, we wander these lands, singin', spinnin' yarns, and foreseein' what's to come."

"Aahhh… Why should I trust the words of a wandering bard? Your songs may be nothing but wind. Your kind, mayhap, will take my coin and give me naught but a song. How do I know that you have something useful for me?"

"Ye don't. But ye be riskin' a mug o' yer finest ale tae discover. 'Tis a wee price tae pay."

"Alright. Mateld! A mug of your best ale for the lady."

"Comin,' Master Undersheriff."

The ale arrived and Alexis drank it down with gusto.

"Now that you've been paid, deliver your goods!"

"Aye. An' so I will, then. So, I will." She picked up her lute, struck a chord and began.

> *"In the shire, a scholar's fate, under moon, envy's hate.*
> *From shadows deep, a student's ire, kindles dark,*
> *the hidden fire.*
> *Silent whispers in the night, wisdom's flame*
> *snuffed out of sight.*

"There ye be, Master Undersheriff. Worth the cost, is it?"

"Maybe. At what cost the second verse?"

Before he could answer one of the undersheriff's constables appeared.

"Yes, constable? What brings you back?"

"Word in the town and other taverns, Master Alric. People say that the murderer is none other than the Devil himself!"

"Nonsense, Constable. Sit and listen to Mistress Alexis' tale. Sing on Mistress."

"Ah, no, Master Undersheriff. Not without me due. This time I'll be havin' another ale, and a piece o' silver for me next song."

"You drive a hard bargain, Mistress Alexis. What should I expect from your song this time?"

"I just told ye who killed the lecturer. If ye didn't catch that, that's no fault o' mine. This time I'll tell ye who killed the shopkeeper."

"You cannot possibly know either killer. Why should I believe you?" But it was clear that Alexis, Bard of the Shire, knew much more than it appeared.

"But I do, Master Undersheriff, I most certainly do. Have we ourselves a bargain then? Mind ye, I've the sight."

"Superstition. Oh, very well, Mistress. Mateld… Another ale. And Constable, listen you carefully to her words." And the undersheriff handed a piece of silver to the bard.

"Yes. Listen ye carefully, and with both yer ears, Master Undersheriff, and ye too, Constable. Listen and ye'll learn.

> *Market square holds silent dread, where father's blood was wrongly shed.*
>
> *By kin's hand, though veiled in night, a bond of blood now torn by spite.*
>
> *In the shop where shadows cling silent, the mallet's fatal ring."*

"What have we learned here, Bard? This tells us nothing that we don't already know."

"That's as may be, Master Undersheriff. But I've given ye the answers to two crimes. And mark ye, there is one more yet to come, and I know who it is and who the killer will be. One more ale and a gold coin this time."

"You are stealing from us, Bard. How do I know that you will deliver? I don't even know that the two I've paid for are true."

"Aye, that's so. But that is for ye to decide. Ye be the undersheriff. I be just a bard. With the sight."

The undersheriff was becoming impatient. This snip of a girl – and a wanderer at that – was taking him. But his curiosity was getting the better of him. Perhaps with this final clue he and his constables could solve two murders and prevent a third. A far-fetched supposition, but just, perhaps. "Very well, bard. Here is your gold but no ale until you sing your song."

"Ah, no, Master Undersheriff. Full payment upfront, so it is. That be our deal."

"Very well, Bard. Mateld! Yet another ale if you please."

"On the way, Master Undersheriff."

"Aye and thank you. Here's your final song," and she finished off her ale and set the mug on the table. Taking up her lute, she began:

> *"Next in line, a sister's fate, through jealousy that turns to hate.*
>
> *A killer's rage, a storm to brew, beneath the moon's cold, watchful view."*

As she sang her song, a bolt from a crossbow flashed past the undersheriff's face and lodged in the bard's neck. Dropping her lute she fell to the floor.

"Constable! Run outside and find who shot that bolt. It was no accident. Hurry, run! I will see to the bard."

Bending over the bard he could see that Alexis was still alive but barely. She reached up and grabbed the undersheriff's collar, pulling him down close to her dying lips. Gasping with her last breath,

"Her light, now dimmed by kin's deceit, a tale of

sorrow, incomplete."

And the bard, finally earning her due and keeping her word as was the custom of her folk, died in a pool of her own blood.

Undersheriff Alric – Following a Clue

Alric, alarmed at the bard's last words, summoned one of his constables, "Keep everyone here. We will need to convene a coroner's jury quickly. Send one of the other constables to fetch the deputy coroner at once." Turning to Mateld, who was standing frozen with shock, "Barmaid, can you write?"

"Yes, master undersheriff. I was taught by my mum who was in service to a fine lady who…"

"Yes, yes. Fetch parchment, quills, and ink. You will be our scribe."

"Yes, Master Undersheriff. Right away."

The undersheriff turned, hearing people entering the inn. "Ahh, Master Deputy Coroner. We have a death and I have assembled your jury. It should take no time at all. There were plenty of witnesses, and the body is here. The cause of death is obvious."

"The jury and I will judge that, Master Undersheriff. Have we a scribe?"

"We do, Master. Mateld, the barmaid, will keep our roll."

"She can write, then?" The deputy coroner seemed surprised.

"Aye, that she can. Educated when her mother was in service to a highborn lady."

"Very well, then. Let us be on with it."

True to the undersheriff's prediction, the inquest was over in under an hour with a verdict of wrongful death by persons unknown at the time.

"Constable, take the body to the caravan on the edge of town. She should be with her people."

"Aye, Master Undersheriff. On our way."

It was just a few miles to the encampment of the travellers, and little time had passed since the murder. Thus, the constables were surprised to find a group from the little community waiting for them at the perimeter of their camp, which contained a collection of tents, carts, and wagons.

An old woman, Alexis' grandmother the constables assumed, walked up to the officers. "Ye be bringin' me mo chuisle? She was me beloved granddaughter. Less than a day in yer cold stone shadows and ye be bringin' me her dead body? If the hand that struck her down is not punished by yer laws, then the winds around us, the earth beneath us, and the spirits of our ancestors will seek revenge. There will be no peace for the soul who has wronged her, not in this life nor the next. Our cries for justice will not be silenced until the murderer is silenced."

"We understand your grief, Mother, and we are doing

what we may to bring your granddaughter's killer to justice."

"Aye. And well ye might! Now tak yer motley band back to yer evil town and leave us to mourn!" Two elderly men from the assembled travelers stepped forward and with gentle reverence placed the body of Alexis, her lute beside her, on a rough cart and transported her back to the encampment. The constables turned and departed whence they came.

The undersheriff was puzzled. How could the killer know that the bard was offering him the solution to the two prior murders? The constables had returned to the inn without apprehending the man with the crossbow but vowing that their fellows were hard at the search, and they expected results soon.

No sooner had the constable reported than two other constables, dragging a scruffy peasant between them, entered the inn. Throwing down a crude crossbow, one of the constables addressed the undersheriff. "Here is the killer, Master. We caught him trying to hide with the murder weapon."

"I have done nothing, yer grace. Why, I just was out looking for a meal. It's been days since I've 'et. Yer lordship."

"Show me your palms, peasant!" The prisoner did so. "I see that you have been firing your crossbow. There is a deep grove in your right palm where you had to pull the bowstring to cock the weapon. Well? Speak, man! What say you?"

"Just outside of town, in that big forest, I was roasting a hare for me dinner."

"That 'big forest' is the woods near Wytham, and it is the king's land. What were you doing roasting a hare there?

Where did you get the hare to roast? Quickly, now. You try my patience!"

Alexis' killer knew he was in trouble. He also knew that he had been caught hunting on the king's land. But they had not yet accused him of killing her. "But, yer grace, how would I know? I am just passing through."

The undersheriff was out of patience. "Constables, take the prisoner to the castle and put him to the question. We will know soon enough of his killings, both hares and bards."

"No! No! Please, yer honor. I'll tell ye all I can."

"And the better for you. Killing game on the king's lands is a hanging offence. So is killing bards in a tavern. You only can hang once, so out with it man, or it's the castle dungeon for you."

"All right." The prisoner's head hung with obvious fear and defeat. Almost silently, he said, "I was huntin' a hare for me dinner. How was I to know that I was on the king's land?"

"Speak up, man! We hardly can hear you." The undersheriff's impatience was obvious.

"Anyway, I left me fire to fetch some water from a nearby stream. When I got back, this wench was runnin' off with me hare. I chased after her but couldna find her. Then I came into town hopin' for a meal, and I saw her. I followed her here, and I shot her. She'll steal no more hares from me." He said no more.

The undersheriff thought for a moment. Could this be the killer of the lecturer and the shopkeeper? He would keep the prisoner locked up until he found out. There always was "the question." Faced with that, the undersheriff was certain he would confess. Sir Henry de Thisteldon, the castellan of Oxford Castle, wherein were the dungeons, also was the high sheriff of Oxfordshire. There would be no difficulty in bringing this killer to pay for his murderous sins. "Take him to the dungeons!"

CHAPTER 17: THE UNVEILING VEIL

Undersheriff Alric still was puzzled. Holding Mateld's parchment loosely in his hand, he studied the song:

> In the shire, a scholar's fate, under moon, envy's hate.

> From shadows deep, a student's ire, kindles dark, the hidden fire.

> Silent whispers in the night, wisdom's flame snuffed out of sight.

> Market square holds silent dread, where father's blood was wrongly shed.

> By kin's hand, though veiled in night, a bond of blood now torn by spite.

> In the shop where shadows cling, silent the mallet's fatal ring.

> Next in line, a sister's fate, through jealousy that turns to hate.

> A killer's rage, a storm to brew, beneath the moon's, watchful view.

> Her light, now dimmed by kin's deceit, a tale of sorrow, incomplete.

Nothing came to mind. It was little but a bard's tale–wind and no more. He had wasted his coins–which out of guilt for being the apparent reason that the bard was killed he sent to her family with her body and lute. But something niggled at the back of his mind and, ever the lawman, Alric the Bald had learned to pay attention when he experienced such a feeling.

Undersheriff Alric – Some Outside Help

The undersheriff was more and more certain that the bard's song held the clues to two murders and a very explicit warning about a third killing. He did not know why he was so certain, but certain he was. "Mateld!! Another ale!"

"Coming, Master Undersheriff."

"Mateld, please make another copy of the bard's song. Here are some coins for your trouble."

"Certainly, Master. Right away." And with the coins jiggling cheerfully in the pouch, or scrip, tied securely around her waist she was off to do her copying.

The undersheriff sipped at his ale waiting for Mateld to finish copying. He recalled vividly one of the things the bard said,

"I just told ye who killed the lecturer. If ye didn't catch that, that's no fault o' mine. This time I'll tell ye who killed the shopkeeper."

As he drank, lost in his own speculations about the song, one of his constables entered the inn. "Greetin's to ye Master Undersheriff. We have learned no more about the wretch what killed the bard. Mayhap, he is tellin' us the truth."

"Mayhap, but not, I'm thinking, the whole truth. Take this song to Lady Beatrix and tell her that at her convenience I beg her help figuring out just what it means."

"Aye, Master. On my way. Should I find you when I am finished?"

"Yes. I want to know what she says."

CHAPTER 18: BURDEN OF TRUTH

In which Sister Agnes struggles with the growing danger of her pursuit and we see the killer's unraveling mental state as clues begin to align against him.

The constable approached the manor house door slowly his steps hesitant with some trepidation. After all, he never had been to the manor of a high-born lady. But orders were orders and as he approached the door a colossal hunting hound burst around the corner of the immense building, its bay echoing fiercely. The overcast sky and a stiff breeze down from the north heightened the impact of the immense, drooling beast before him.

The constable froze in fear. This was the biggest hound he had ever seen, and it sounded hungry. The constable did not want to be its meal but just then the manor door opened and an older man, obviously one of the servants by his attire, stood in the doorway.

"Thorold! Down!" The dog sat instantly at the man's command. "And what would ye be wantin,' Constable?"

"I have a message for Lady Beatrix from Undersheriff Alric, Master."

"I be no master, Constable. I be Samuel, her ladyship's footman. I'll see if she can see you. Wait here. Thorold! Guard!" And the footman disappeared behind the big oak door, the huge hound sitting at attention watching the constable's every move.

Beatrix – The Song

Before long, an impatient Lady Beatrix opened the door.

"Enter, Constable, and tell what you have for me that is so important."

Stepping inside, "Thank you m'lady. Alexis, a young bard, sang a song for Master Alric claiming that it was the solution to two murders and the warning of a third. Before she could finish singing her song, she was killed by a bolt from a crossbow. But she was able to whisper the last line to the undersheriff with her dying breath. He wrote the song on this parchment, or, rather, he told it to Mateld, the barmaid, who wrote it. But he does not ken its meaning. He begs your insights, m'lady."

Beatrix now was becoming curious. "Well, give me the song, and I'll look at it, but I cannot promise to be much immediate help for your master." Beatrix read the words on the parchment, her expression darkening as she read each line, her brows tightening and her mouth forming a thin line of consternation. "Tell me exactly how this event occurred, Constable. I would know exactly how the song came to be and what you know of the person who murdered the bard." Her impatience was palpable, shifting quickly to focused concern as she read the lines over several times.

Slowly, the constable repeated the story in as much detail as he could recall. As he spoke, Beatrix's eyes never left his face. Such was her concentration that, even in the darkening gloom of the late afternoon, her eyes never blinked. When he finished, Beatrix closed her eyes, clearly in deep concentration on the song and the constable's story. When she opened them again, she had a message for the constable to take to his undersheriff.

"I cannot unravel this myself. There are pieces that are obscure. I must have assistance. Tell your master that I am taking the song to Sister Agnes at the Abbey. She certainly will be able to offer insight. You may go now and return to the undersheriff with my message. I will keep the parchment and will away to the abbey with it immediately."

Without another word to the constable, she summoned her footman. "Samuel! Escort the constable to the door and see to Thorold. Then have my groom fetch the carriage and be ready to take me to the abbey at once."

Having given her instructions, she turned and disappeared up the ornate curving staircase leading to her chambers.

Sister Agnes – The Riddle of The Song

In the shire, a scholar's fate, under moon, envy's hate.

From shadows deep, a student's ire, kindles dark, the hidden fire.

Silent whispers in the night, wisdom's flame snuffed out of sight.

Market square holds silent dread, where father's blood was wrongly shed.

By kin's hand, though veiled in night, a bond of blood now torn by spite.

In the shop where shadows cling, silent the mallet's fatal ring.

Next in line, a sister's fate, through jealousy that turns to hate.

A killer's rage, a storm to brew, beneath the moon's cold, watchful view.

Her light, now dimmed by kin's deceit, a tale of sorrow, incomplete.

"Verily, this bard was privy to matters deep and dark. She tells us more through her rhymes than words alone might convey. Her song, though seemingly direct, cloaks truths in layers of allusion."

Lady Beatrix pondered Sister Agnes' words, a furrow of concern etching her brow. "To mine eyes, the song's message appeared straightforward. Yet there is much revealed with each subsequent reading. Its clarity dims, and shadows grow. It is curious and confounding."

"Aye, milady, and therein lies our challenge," Sister Agnes mused, her fingers idly tracing the edges of the parchment. "It appears on the surface that the bard's verses suggest both victims were known to their aggressor. Our own inquiries confirm that. Yet, the connection between these two souls eludes us still. The relationship or common thread that binds their fates remains an enigma. I need time to pray and ponder this new development."

"Very well, Sister. I will be on my way, then. I want to get back to the manor before dark."

"God go with you, my lady."

"And with you, Sister."

Sister Agnes examined the parchment laid out upon her worktable; her brow furrowed in concentration. The words of the bard's song, though seemingly straightforward, hid a deeper message, as if shrouded in the mists of dawn. She inspected the verses individually, pondering them as if they were pieces of a puzzle, each holding a secret to be unlocked.

"Each stanza seems a riddle cloaked in allegory," she mused. The task at hand was not merely one of curiosity, but a challenge, each line a thread in the fabric of the complete song, and, as well, of the mystery. Could there be a pattern, a recurring idea or symbol that twisted and turned through the lines, elusive yet always present? Such insights, mayhap, might illuminate new paths, guiding her through the labyrinth of the verses to the core of the message hidden within.

Agnes decided that her first endeavour would be to seek out any uniformity or shared imagery that might connect one verse to the next. In this she was not merely a scholar but a seeker of truth delving into the depths of the bard's song to unearth the message concealed within. She began with the first verse:

In the shire, a scholar's fate, under moon, envy's hate.

From shadows deep, a student's ire, kindles dark, the hidden fire.

Silent whispers in the night, wisdom's flame snuffed out of sight.

This verse clearly described Thomas' murder. As she contemplated the verse in front of her, she noted two interesting themes: *a scholar's fate* pointed to Thomas the lecturer and *a student's ire* seemed to incriminate one of the lecturer's students. Dismissing the rest of the verse as shadows, hiding its true meaning. Agnes took a piece of parchment and a quill. Dipping the quill into her ink pot, she copied down her observations.

Agnes put the quill down and reached again for the parchment containing the bard's whole song:

Market square holds silent dread, where father's blood was wrongly shed.

By kin's hand, though veiled in night, a bond of blood now torn by spite.

In the shop where shadows cling, silent the mallet's fatal ring.

Weariness beginning to engulf her she called for her novice. "Isabel! I need your assistance. Please join me in my workroom."

"Aye, Sister. How may I serve you?"

"Please fetch your writing tools and a parchment or two. I need a scribe."

"Of course, Sister. I will be right back."

As Agnes sat back in her straight-backed wooden chair, she rubbed her eyes, attempting to drive the fatigue away. Her respite was brief, however, as Isabel returned with a tray holding her ink pots and quill pens. She sat down at the small worktable where she routinely scribed the notes of Sister Agnes' examinations. Agnes handed her the parchment upon which she had written the two not regarding the first verse:

A scholar's fate pointed to Thomas the lecturer, and *a student's ire* seemed to incriminate one of the lecturer's students.

"Take you these notes, Isabel, and add what else I may tell you." She went back to examining the second verse. Again, two parts of the verse stood out: *where father's blood was wrongly shed* and *by kin's hand*. "Isabel, add this to my notes:" and she quoted the fragments of the verse that revealed themselves as important.

Again, Agnes sat back, her eyes closed, imagining the connection between the two verses. The connection struck like lightning. Sitting up straight, her eyes wide she turned to her novice.

"Isabel, write you down this. It is important. The killer was a student related in some way to the butcher. Moreover, the *student's ire* and *a bond of blood now torn by spite* suggest strong emotional motives. That bears witness to our findings at the autopsies. We know now where to look for the killer. It is clear now that the three verses each represent a murder. But we have but two murders so far. Does that mean that a third murder is yet to come?"

"Sister… if you peer too closely, you could be in great danger."

"You are correct, of course, Isabel, but I shall take care and ask the Lord for protection. Ours is a divine task. God will help us to solve the mystery and will keep us safe as we search if we but seek His guidance."

The Killer – Returning to the Mage

The killer gazed at the palm of his hand where the mage had placed the amulet. Although it had been but a few days since his visit, the killer saw that the fiery welts were disappearing, leaving only white scares.

"They know," he thought. "They know and they will come for me. I must see Master Wystan at once! He must help me…" The killer waited impatiently until dark and then sneaked from the gate of the town, pointing his steps rapidly toward the crossroads and the huge ominous mansion nearby.

Arriving at the crossroads, the killer slowed his steps and surveyed the road and nearby bushes for any onlookers. Then, carefully, keeping well back from the road itself, the killer started for the mansion. He had taken but a few steps when the mage's manservant approached him, some irritation evident in his tone. "And what is it now that you need?"

The killer responded, shrill panic in his voice; "I must see your master. I am sure that they know, and I need protection. The amulet is fading, and I am frightened." He lifted his hand, palm up, and showed the old manservant the healing scars.

"I will see what can be arranged. Wait you here."

Moments later the manservant returned. Looking wearily at the killer, "I suppose if you must see the master, you must. Attend me, and we will go to his workroom. However, ye ken that ye have but little time with the master. He is very busy." The killer followed, close by the old servant, every nerve taught, his eyes darting about for any witness, his breath coming in short panting gasps.

The killer could not say how long they walked or where they entered the ancient mansion. All he knew was that he found himself in the mage's workroom, Master Wystan standing within the magic circle that he had so recently drawn.

"Yes!? Yes!? What is it that you want, young master? My time is valuable. We have a bargain, you, and I, and you know that I will not let you out of it. So it must be that you require additional protection. Well? Speak up, boy, and be quick about it." Wystan's voice seemed to roar, to fill the room to overflowing. The killer could even see the tendrils of smoke rising from the censers placed around the room dancing to the sound.

"I am afraid, Master. They know!! They know everything! I need more protection, or they will find me and kill me. Help me, Master! Help me!"

"Pshaw!" The mage was smiling a wicked-looking grin. I will help you. But we had a bargain, did we not? If you want my help, you must pay the price. And the price has come due. Do you not agree, Young Master?"

"Anything, Master. Anything. Just help me!"

"What makes you think, assuming as I am asked to believe, that you *can* think, that you are found out?" The mage's words were not kind. He was mocking the killer, and the killer knew it.

"I have someone. She knows all. She works with the people investigating my work. She has told me of a bard who knew all before she was killed. The bard told the undersheriff, and they will come for me."

"But you did not kill the bard. So, they will search out her killer and you will be safe. Now, leave me to my work!" The roaring voice again.

"No, Master! No! There is more. The person I know who is close to the investigation of the two murders told me. They know! They have figured the bard's song. The song tells the story." The killer was on his knees now, begging.

"Oh, well. I suppose that I must, or I never shall be shut of you." The mage clearly was exasperated. "Very well. I shall give you a potion and when you awake, you will be safe. But it is time to pay my due. You have killed twice. If they do find you out, they can hang you but once. So, you will kill again."

"Anything, Master. Anything." And the mage gave the potion telling the killer what he must do. As the mage had predicted, the killer awoke again in the crossroads. He was weary. Weary to death. He wanted only to sleep. He crawled off to the bushes by the side of the road, and like some feral animal, slept the sleep of the dead.

Sister Agnes awoke with a start. She had been tired, oh, so tired when she retired after evening prayers. But something had disturbed her sleep enough to awake her abruptly. Perspiration was pouring down her face and her hands were shaking. She dressed quickly and made for the chapel. She had no doubt that God was calling her. But in this she was mistaken.

As she prayed at her prie-dieu in the chapel she was overcome by a vision of Mother Mary. "You are gathering the correct information, Agnes. But you are not connecting what you see. Go back and look again. There is one clue that will solve your mystery. Make haste, Agnes. The killer you seek knows that you are finding him out and is seeking aid from dark forces."

"Holy Mother, what must I do to see these connections of which you speak?"

"That you must find out for yourself. But you must not tarry. The killer knows and may come for you. I will protect you as I can, but everything now is in your hands and the hands of the Father. Pray and seek the truth. You will see it then." And the Holy Mother was gone leaving Agnes exhausted. She worked her way back to her chamber and climbed back into bed without even removing her habit. In seconds, she was asleep.

CHAPTER 19: BENEATH THE MOON'S GAZE

In which we observe a suspenseful encounter between Sister Agnes and the killer, though his identity remains veiled.

Sister Agnes awoke realizing that she had missed both Matins and breakfast. She felt as if she had not slept at all, but also a sense of purpose overcame her. Vividly she recalled the visit by Holy Mary and Her message. What she could not understand was the clue that the Holy Virgin offered.

Changing from yesterday's habit into a fresh robe and tunic, Agnes went first to the chapel. After an hour of meditation and prayers imploring the Blessed Virgin to offer further clues, she arose and walked slowly around the inner wall to her workroom where Isabel was waiting.

Agnes – The Edge of Discovery

"Sister Agnes… there's a message for you from Brother Ambrose at Rewley Abbey."

Agnes read the message, her expression turning to one of puzzlement. "That is odd. Why could he possibly want me? He is asking to meet at the entrance arch of Godstow after Compline. Such an unusual request."

"But he seems quite urgent about it."

"Forsooth, that much is clear. Well then, tonight it is, after Compline. The moon will be up, so the meeting should be safe enough."

"Why are you concerned about Brother Ambrose, Sister?"

"It is just so out of the ordinary, and it's not like a monk from Rewley to be out after dark. Plus, how does he plan to get into Godstow at that time?"

"There's one more thing, Sister Agnes." Isabel looked slightly uneasy. "Lady Beatrix is in the garden awaiting you, if you find it convenient."

"Of course. I must go to her right away. We have puzzles to solve, and with her help, mayhap we will make some progress."

As she walked toward the gardens in the interior of the abbey walls, Agnes read and reread the note from Ambrose. She could not be certain, but the writing and the tone of the missive did not seem to her as coming from the monk, especially from a monk whom she hardly knew. "Of course, he was a close friend to Thomas, the lecturer. And," she mused, "why late at night after compline? A conundrum yet again. 'Enigmas wrapped in mysteries'."

As she entered the shelter of the gardens, Lady Beatrix rose to meet her. "I have some thoughts about the bard's song."

"Well, my lady, I certainly hope that you have progressed farther than I. So far, I cannot make much out of it. And," she continued, "I wonder how she came about the knowledge that she claims the song reveals."

"That is what I wondered. But look you here:" Beatrix opened the parchment with the song written upon.

> *Market square holds silent dread, where father's blood was wrongly shed.*
> *By kin's hand, though veiled in night, a bond of*

blood now torn by spite.

In the shop where shadows cling, silent the mallet's fatal ring.

"Look you closely at the first two lines, Sister. They strongly suggest that the killer was related to the butcher."

"Indeed, they do, my lady. In fact, they suggest that the killer of the butcher was his son. But how could the bard know this?"

"That is a difficult question. But the implication is clear. What I cannot yet fathom is how it connects to the other killing or the prediction of a third."

"Then let us ask, *cui bono*? Who benefits by the death of the butcher?"

"Nobody, Sister. Or, at least, I can see nobody who benefits directly. From what I've been able to find, the son has no interest in inheriting the butcher shop. It all goes to his younger sister in the event of the butcher's passing. Could she be our killer?"

"I doubt that my lady. The blow that killed the butcher was dealt by the strong arm of a person slightly taller than the victim. The daughter does not fit that description. Also, if we assume that the same killer dispatched both the butcher and the lecturer, where is the connection between the daughter and the lecturer? By all accounts, the lecturer sought naught but a quiet life at his college. He had no interest in any woman that we have been able to find."

Beatrix ruminated a while over the questions that the conversation had raised. "Sister, mayhap there is a relationship that as yet we know naught of."

Agnes pulled the note from the monk from the sleave of her tunic. "Look you at this, my lady. What meaning does it convey to you?"

Beatrix took the offered message and looked at it closely. "There is something wrong, here, Sister. I have met Brother Ambrose at the inquest for the lecturer. This does not sound like him from my recollection."

Isabel, who had been standing behind the ladies became increasingly nervous. "May I go back to the workroom, Sister? I have much to do before Vespers."

Agnes seemed distracted. "Of course, Isabel. I will see you at Vespers." And Isabel left hurriedly, and Agnes returned to perusing the note from Ambrose.

"Well, my lady, it appears that the only way to solve the riddle of Ambrose's note is to wait for Compline. I shall pray for wisdom from the Holy Mother." And Agnes related the story of her vision to Beatrix.

"It would be well to have help from Above, Sister. I am uncomfortable with the way things stand."

"As am I, my lady, but the way to truth does not always have a safe path. There is something dark here, I know, but I cannot discern it yet."

Wishing Agnes Godspeed and, again, admonishing care, Beatrix left her standing in the gardens alone.

Agnes – The Encounter

It was all Agnes could do to keep her mind on Compline.

As her sister nuns chanted, *Deus, in adjutorium meum intende* imploring the assistance of God, Agnes contemplated her meeting with the monk. Her heartfelt, *Domine, ad adjuvandum me festina* begged the Lord to make haste to protect her, seeming especially apt. With the final *In manus tuas, Domine*, Sister Agnes placed herself in

God's hands and, prayers completed, she left the chapel walking along the inner wall to the arch with no small amount of trepidation.

The moon was high, but clouds conspired to block its rays. Standing in the dark of the arch, her fear became increasingly overwhelming. She gripped the rosary attached to her girdle and, clutching it tightly, invoked the protection of Mary. As she prayed, her hands shaking, she heard a voice.

"You are a fool, Sister Agnes." A man's voice but certainly not the monk's. Her worst fears realized, she responded in a tremulous voice, "and why might that be, pray tell?"

"Because you are here. And because you seek a killer who might kill you as well." The voice came from the shadows, but Agnes had no desire to see who owned it.

"And why would he want to kill me?" She clutched her rosary tighter.

"Because you know too much, and he will not let you live with that knowledge."

"And how will he come to me. The abbey is well-guarded."

"I am here, am I not? I have no business with the abbey or its persons and, yet, here I am. If I was the killer you seek, you might be dead in a moment. But for now, Sister, this is just a warning. Cease your foolish "investigating" and get back to your workroom, caring for your sisters. And, when again you talk to Lady Beatrix, warn her as well. I have little patience and stronger gods than yours protect me. Now, Begone!"

Shaking, Agnes left the arch without hesitation. She went directly to the chapel to pray for strength. As she prayed, she became aware of a soothing, protective presence. Looking up towards the alter, she saw again the vision of Mother Mary.

"Agnes, you are not foolish. Nobody who seeks truth is foolish. But you and Lady Beatrix are in real danger. You must warn her, and you must continue your search. But, Agnes, you also must have a care. The killer has killed twice, and he will kill again. No person and no place are out of his reach." And the vision faded as Agnes, trembling and with tears in her eyes, thought over and over Mary's last words: *No person and no place are out of his reach.*

As she returned to her room, her rosary clutched in her hand, she suddenly recalled something else Mary had said: *The killer has killed twice, and he will kill again.* A clue! The Holy Mother had revealed an important clue; the killer of the lecturer was the same who killed the butcher. *And he will kill again.*

CHAPTER 20: THE CRUMBLING VEIL

In which we see Sister Agnes and Lady Beatrix solving the Riddle of the Song, anticipating another murder, and closing in on the killer's identity which, when revealed, leads to a confrontation during which the killer is captured. Deceit from an unexpected quarter is revealed.

Sister Agnes summoned her novice. "Isabel, please get word to Lady Beatrix that I must see her at once."

"Aye, Sister. I think that the boy who delivers bread for the kitchen is here. He can get the message to her."

"Very well. Ask him to be quick about it, and if he gives this note to the lady, she will pay him for his trouble, and gladly." Agnes handed a note to Isabel who left the workroom to find the delivery boy. Now, all Agnes could do was wait. She did not have long. Before afternoon prayers, Lady Beatrix was in the workroom.

"What has happened that ye called me so urgently, Sister?"

"I believe that I almost have solved the Riddle of the Song and I need your help to finish."

Agnes and Beatrix – The Riddle of the Song

"My lady, thank you for coming so quickly. I have had another vision of the Blessed Virgin. She gave us a clue. She was talking about the killer, and she said, '*The killer has killed twice, and he will kill again.*' He will kill again.

Recall the last verse of the song:

> *Next in line, a sister's fate, through jealousy that turns to hate.*
>
> *A killer's rage, a storm to brew, beneath the moon's cold, watchful view.*
>
> *Her light, now dimmed by kin's deceit, a tale of sorrow, incomplete.*

"A sister's fate. After meeting the voice in the moon light, I was sure that meant me." And Sister Agnes recounted the meeting on that dark night. "But that was not what the song meant. Now I am certain."

"Sister, you have found the answer. The sister is a real sister, not one of your community. And look you at the last line:

> *Her light, now dimmed by kin's deceit, a tale of sorrow, incomplete.*

"… 'by kin's deceit.' This can be but one person."

"We must alert the undersheriff and go with all haste to his sister's house. Go you with all speed my lady. He may already have killed her." Beatrix was away. Mounting her pony, she raced toward town and Undersheriff Alric. As she arrived at the small building that served as office, sleeping quarters and gaol, one of the undersheriff's constables met her.

"And how is it that you are here, and in such a hurry, too, m'lady?"

"Constable, I must see the undersheriff at once. It is urgent."

"Of course. Attend me. He is just inside."

It took Beatrix just two minutes to convey her message and for the undersheriff to call for several of his men. "Constable, fetch Constable George. He is the best archer in the shire. Tell him to bring his arbalest. We may have need of him."

Together the little party headed straight for the butcher shop where Isabella of Shrewsbury lived with her mother, Lady Elinore.

The Killer – Confronting the Undersheriff

As the undersheriff and his party stormed through the door of the empty shop, they heard screaming from the floor above. A woman's voice, "Please, oh please, Gilbert! You must not do this terrible thing."

"Silence, mother! I have been commanded by Lord Saturn to send him the body of my sister. I dare not disobey. She is the perfect sacrifice. Now never will she usurp my rightful place as the head of this family. Never!" And Gilbert, the killer of his father and the lecturer, raised his blade to strike.

Standing quietly behind Beatrix, the undersheriff, and the rest of his men, Constable George quietly raised his arbalest and as Gilbert's hand descended, grasping the knife destined for his sister's heart, the constable released his bolt. The bolt covered the short distance in less than a second and found its mark in Gilbert's wrist. The knife fell to the floor and Gibert, howling in pain, tried to extract the bolt from his wrist.

Isabell, unhurt, fell to the floor senseless from her ordeal. Beatrix rushed to her and, raising Isabella's head, called for water. She dipped her kerchief in the water and began wiping gently at Isabella's face and forehead. Before long Isabella was awake and, seeing that it was a highborn lady tending her just as if she was one of her own children, tried to jump to her feet.

"Oh, my lady, you must not do that. I am but a shop girl, fit only to serve you. You must not serve me so."

"Pshaw! You are the daughter of your noble mother. We are the same, Isabella, you and I.. Now, if you can stand, we will sit you in that chair until you feel better. Constable George, please, a cup of ale for Lady Isabella."

"Yes, my lady. At once."

Gilbert, grasping his painfully injured wrist, raged at the undersheriff and his men. "You have done for me cur of a law dog." Turning to Beatrix, "Harpy!! This is your doing. You and that meddling nun!"

He took a deep breath and, slowly realizing that his sister was alive and unharmed, Gilbert scowled and stared straight into her eyes, "Usurper. Now you think that you will have what is rightfully mine. Never!!!!"

Invoking the spirits he had heard called upon by Wystan the Sage, he shouted, with his eyes now glazed over and looking skyward, "Saturn, Caimon, Haron, Azathor, Zarathos and all of your avenging spirits, I conjure you to call down the fires of Hell upon Isabella, falsely called "Lady Isabella," who is the usurper of my place and fortune!"

Isabella shrunk back in fear, her ale forgotten in Gilbert's onslaught.

Beatrix walked straight to Gilbert and, inches from his face Beatrix met his glare. "Blasphemer! Your words have no power here. God's light conquers all darkness. His justice is not swayed by your curses. You cannot harm those under His protection. Your soul is in peril, Blasphemer. You will answer for your deeds and your false gods cannot protect you."

Then, looking straight at Isabella, her voice firm but gentle. "The Lord is our refuge and strength. No curse, no matter how dark, can break through His light. Remember that God is with you. No evil can stand against His will.

I have examined your family, Isabella. Your true father, and that of your sister, Isabel, was not whom you thought.

Lady Elinore was married to a noble knight. When your mother's family fell on hard times, your father joined a body of knights bound for the Crusades. He believed that there were riches to be had in the Holy Land. Sadly, he was killed leaving your mother with two girls to bring up. You and Isabel are, indeed, of noble birth."

Gilbert – The Confession

The undersheriff and two of his constables ushered Gilbert to the goal, just a short walk from the butcher shop.

"Constable George, go ye and fetch Master Jonas, the barber-surgeon. It would seem this braggart has sustained an injury. In sooth, I cannot imagine whence it came." The undersheriff met with loud guffaws, particularly from Constable George, from the constables, but none such from Gilbert, still howling and cursing his pain.

The undersheriff approached Gilbert, unmindful of his wails. "Well, me boy, seems you have a problem." The undersheriff took hold of the bolt, still embedded in Gilbert's hand, and gave it a slight twist. His move was met with more and louder wails of pain from Gilbert. The remaining constables looked on in silence.

Suddenly the wails ceased. A look of rage replaced the pain on Gilbert's face, and he looked straight into Master Alric's eyes. His voice was softened, low-pitched and powerful.

"Cur! I curse you in the name of Lord Saturn and all his infernal minions! It was in his name I slew that miserly old wretch who kept his wealth hidden and that self-righteous prig of a lecturer who believed he was wiser than all. And in Lord Saturn's name, you, too, will die." With that Gilbert spat in the undersheriff's face, looked away, and his wailing began anew.

Alric was no stranger to aggressive criminals. This was just a minor inconvenience. Wiping his face with his sleeve, he grinned at Gilbert and gave the bolt another little twist just as the barber-surgeon and Constable George entered the goal.

"Well, Master Alric, it seems your prisoner has been injured. I shall attend him."

"You see correctly, Master Surgeon. This beast has found himself at odds with a hunter, who it appears mistook him for game. Can you ease his pain?"

"Indeed, I can." The surgeon snapped off one end of the bolt and extracted the remaining piece from the wound. Gilbert's screams grew louder as the surgeon extracted the bolt. He applied a thick yellow salve to both sides of the wound and bound it with a strip of linen. "That should do for now. Be mindful that no black humors seep from the wound."

Undersheriff Alric – The Old Mansion

The undersheriff turned to Constable George. "Fetch you the lady Beatrix and then meet us at the old mansion by the crossroads. 'Tis there that this murderer claims he was treated by the mage. I would meet this mage and see what he may tell us of Master Gilbert here. The lady, mayhap, can help us get to the truth of things."

"Aye, Master. On my way."

The sun was signalling high noon when the undersheriff, his constables, and Lady Beatrix converged at the crossroads. "Greetings, my lady. Thank you for helping us get to the truth of these murders before we turn Master Gilbert over to the courts."

"I am happy to assist, Master Alric. Shall we continue while the sun is high?"

As they approached the mansion the undersheriff noted something strange. "My lady, this mansion does not appear lived-in." Taking the brass lion's head knocker firmly, he pounded loudly on the door. There was no answer. Once more, and still there was no answer. The undersheriff took hold of the door's entry handle and pushed. The old door opened easily, albeit with the squeaks of age and neglect.

The party stepped slowly into the room. The floor was coated with dust. Lady Beatrix started to examine the room carefully. "Master Alric, if thee may, please keep you and your men back from this room whilst I look more closely."

Walking carefully and slowly around the edges of the large entryway, Lady Beatrix observed, "This entryway has seen nary a footfall in many a long year. Look you, Master Alric… the dust throughout the room and on the floor has not been disturbed. Let us follow that hall but stay thee behind me."

At the end of the hallway, a closed door blocked their way. "Keep thee back, Master Undersheriff. I would examine what we find on the other side of this door." Beatrix slowly twisted the doorknob and gently pushed the heavy oak door open. She was greeted again by layers of dust. And, again, she walked slowly about the walls of the old room, looking at the walls, empty shelves, and the floor.

"Look you, Master Undersheriff. This room has been used much more recently than the entry hall. See that the dust is much thinner here – perhaps only a week or two old. And the center of the floor seems to have had a drawing of some kind. Ahh… it appears to have been a magic circle. We begin to shed some light on this puzzle."

Continuing her perambulation, she stopped at a place where the dust on the edge of the circle had been disturbed recently. Looking around the faint outline of the circle, she noted a censer, exactly opposite the disturbed dust before her. Continuing around the circle she came to the censer.

"Ahh, Master Undersheriff, look you here. 'Tis the remains of some aromatic herb still in this censer. We must take these to Sister Agnes. She will know what they are. There is a door at the end of this room, which looks like a workroom or something of that ilk. Let us see where the door leads."

Beatrix carefully opened the door and was met with bright sunlight. "This is how the mage entered and left the workroom without using the entry hall. And look you… there are tracks of a large wagon of some sort in the damp soil. We must go at once to Sister Agnes so that she can examine these herbs."

Sister Agnes – The Herbs

Sister Agnes was puzzled. She examined Beatrix's find with her magnifying stone but could not make sense of what she saw. Worse, there was an odour about the herbs that was faintly – but not quite completely – familiar. As she separated intact leaves from the burnt ashes, she became increasingly muddled. In fact, something was beginning to make her head swim, yet she could not identify the cause. She stepped away from her worktable to contemplate what she saw.

As she crossed the work room to Beatrix and the undersheriff, her head, strangely, began to clear. "My lady, this is a strange herb, indeed. Its fumes affect the mind. We must send for Elias of Warwick, the apothecary whom I consult on matters such as this."

"Sister, we shan't wait a moment," the undersheriff spoke firmly. "Constable George, go ye to the apothecary shop in town and fetch Master Elias at once. Tell him he is needed most urgently."

"Aye, Master Alric. At once."

It was not long. Agnes knew that Master Elias could not resist an urgent call to the abbey to see his colleague, Agnes.

"And what may I be doin' for ye, Sister?" His Irish brogue always asserted itself when he was excited. And there was no question about his excitement now. "Always when ye call me it's for a fascinatin' problem ye need solved. So, what is it today?"

"It is these herbs, Master Elias. They look strange and they have an odor that scrambles my mind when I breath it in. What do you suppose they are?"

The apothecary examined the remains of the herbs using Agnes' magnifying stone. Then he began to shake his head vigorously, stepping back rapidly from the worktable.

"Aye, Sister. 'Tis not just an herb ye have here, but a mix of two potent herbs, henbane and datura. Where on this round earth did ye find it?"

"It was used to poison the mind of a young man. He believed that he was the servant of Saturn and, in Saturn's name he killed two and almost three. The fumes were administered by one who calls himself a mage. Lady Beatrix found this at an old mansion where it appears the mage mixed his magic potions."

"Nay. 'Tis not uncommon, sister. Those who would cast themselves as magicians or sorcerers often use mixtures of herbs to befuddle their victims. This is henbane and datura, a very potent mix, indeed. They also might use belladonna and mandrake, although this mixture is much more potent."

Beatrix was puzzled. "But how can the mage administer these potent fumes without themselves succumbing?"

"These are very dangerous concoctions, m'lady. The mage and anyone working with him must expose themselves to the fumes– starting with a very small amount and increasing slowly–for a year. They make a ritual of it. At the end of the year, they are immune to the fumes and can administer them, usually in some sort of magical circle, in safety. They believe that demons have entered their bodies giving them immense power."

Agnes listened thoughtfully. "Master Alric, clearly this is what affected Master Gilbert. However, he told us that he committed the first two murders at Lord Saturn's command. That cannot be so. He did not visit the mage until after the second murder. He did those two killings alone without supernatural aid."

"'Twould not be strange for your young man to be confused, Sister. These two herbs can change the way a person sees everything."

Agnes thanked the apothecary, who was grateful for such an unusual request, and the undersheriff. She waited in her work room with Beatrix as they departed.

"We have most of the answers, my lady. Now, we should let the undersheriff decide what to do next. I believe that we have made our contribution."

"In sooth, Sister. We know who, we know how, and we know why. But I fear our job is not done. He has been captured but not yet brought to justice."

Lady Beatrix had no idea how true her words were.

Isabel – A Troubling Confession

Sister Agnes was seated at her worktable concentrating on the potion that she was mixing for one of her sisters who suffered distress breathing. Her concentration was so complete that she did not hear as Isabel, her novice, entered the room, slowly and with head bowed.

"I must speak with you, Sister. I can carry this burden no longer."

Agnes looked up from her potion and scribbled a note on the parchment in front of her. "What can it be that is so heavy a burden, child? You look sorely troubled."

"Lady Rosamund has come to me again in a dream. She says that I must lift this burden, but I fear doing so."

"And what is this burden that you can no longer bear to carry or yet dispose of?"

Isabel turned away from Agnes, not able to meet her eyes as she spoke in a whisper. "I am the cause of the lecturer's death."

"How can this be, Sister? The killer was Gilbert. He has confessed."

"Gilbert is my half-brother, Sister Agnes. I wrote and sent the note that summoned the lecturer to his death."

In which we observe the confession of Isabel and the killer's trials.

Sister Agnes was speechless for several moments. Then, "This is very serious, Sister. We must consult Mother Alice. You have committed a grave sin, and we must decide what to do."

"I fear the worst, Sister. I well know how serious this is, but Gilbert is my half-brother. He flies into a rage when he is turned down. Besides being his half-sister, I fear him greatly. He is one of the reasons that I sought the safety of the convent."

"Still, Isabel, we must seek the wisdom of the abbess and you will confess your sin when the father confessor arrives next week."

"As you say, Sister Agnes. I must relieve myself of this burden. I must beg God's forgiveness and the forgiveness of Mother."

"Go to the chapel and pray for forgiveness. The Lord is a forgiving God. He will hear your prayers. Come back here before evening prayers and I will summon Mother the hear your story and decide how to assist you in removing your pain."

Isabel – A Novice's Sad Story

It was an hour before Vespers when Mother Alice entered Agnes' workroom. "I fear that I have some very difficult news, Mother."

"And what might that be, Sister?"

"Isabel has confessed to me that she wrote the letter that lured the lecturer to his death. She is sorely troubled, but now that Gilbert is in custody of the undersheriff, she feels safe in telling here tale."

"And why would she feel unsafe, Sister?"

"Gilbert, the killer, is her half-brother. She fears him greatly. I have sent for her to come here, tell her story, and beg your mercy."

"Very well. I am ready to hear what she may say." At that moment, a very forlorn Isabel, tears streaming down her face, entered the workroom. "And, so, child, what have you to tell me?"

Isabel gathered herself together and began her tale. "My mother is a high-born lady. She married as a young girl to a brave and noble knight. My sister, Isabella, and I were born of that marriage. My father went on a quest to add to the family's coffers since the fields were bare and our fortunes were dwindling. He never returned and, learning of his death my mother married again, to our stepfather the butcher. While he was not of noble birth, he was quite wealthy and was a well-respected businessman.

From that union came Gilbert. He always was moody and sometimes violent." Isabel stopped, the tears starting anew. Agnes wiped her tears away with a linen napkin. "You must stop, Isabel, and collect yourself. When you are ready, continue."

"Yes Sister. I think I can continue. Gilbert was lazy. He failed many of his courses at Baliol and spent his time and Father's money gambling, drinking, and wenching. Father saw that Gilbert, though he was the oldest, could never take over the family shop, so he made my sister his heir and disinherited Gilbert.

At the same time, one of his fellow scholars, Thomas of Hereford, completed his studies at the top of his class. He was offered the position of Lecturer at Baliol, and was enrolled in the Master's classes. Gilbert was enraged with jealousy over these two events. He swore vengeance.

He came to me and insisted I help him. He had found the secret door that we sisters sometimes use to leave the convent. He told me what to write to Thomas and said that if I did not, he would come back and kill me but only after he killed my beloved mother and Sister Agnes. I had to write the letter and find one of the delivery boys to deliver it. I did so.

I have had horrible dreams of Lady Rosamund, and I could no longer bear them. I came to Sister Agnes and told her what I had done."

Mother Alice listened calmly to Isabel's story. When the novice was finished, the abbess sat in silent contemplation. After a time, she addressed Isabel.

"Your story is touching and disturbing, Sister, and I can well understand how you must have suffered. When you wrote the letter, did you know that its purpose was to lure the lecturer to his death?"

"No, Mother, although, sadly, I was not surprised when I heard. Gilbert is such a violent.... child."

"I must consider this, Isabel. It is very serious, and I must pray the Lord for guidance. Meanwhile, you will continue your duties, attend to your prayers and confess Sunday when Father Confessor is here. Then we will decide what you shall do next. I, too, will pray and consult with the confessor, and, although your confession is a sacred trust between you and your confessor, he can well advise me on what should be done. Now, it is time for

Vespers, and we must away."

Undersheriff Alric
– A Dispute Arises with The Archdeacon

The sun had barely risen over Oxford town when a page accosted the door of the undersheriff. "And why might ye be causin' such a disturbance, boy? It is not yet time for the day's business to start."

"Ye be summoned to the castle on orders from Sheriff Thisteldon and he said to tell ye that ye must come without delay."

"Very well, lad. Tell him that I will be there anon." The undersheriff placed a coin in the boy's hand and closed the door.

Alric the Bald presented himself at the gate of Oxford Castle. St. George's Tower reflected the early morning sun from its stone walls. The damp of the morning dew made the draw bridge a bit slick, and there were guards in chain mail armour flanking the portcullis guarding the castle's entry. The guards, recognizing the undersheriff, snapped to attention and raised the iron portcullis. Alric nodded to them and entered the entryway to the castle.

Here, again, two guards in chain mail flanked heavy door that was, now that the portcullis was dropped, the only way out of the barbican, the space between the portcullis and the oaken door that was the last barrier. Alric glanced around and noted the arrow slits in the wall above. He shivered a bit. Alric always was the bravest of the sheriff's men, still, being trapped in the barbican in this way he found disturbing.

His discomfort did not last long, however. After

acknowledging him, the guards opened the door, and the undersheriff was free to enter. On the other side of the door, a constable awaited his arrival. "Master Undersheriff, I am ordered to escort you to the sheriff's study. Follow me, please."

The pair crossed into the entry hall, and thence through another oaken door, this one studded with decorative iron fittings. Down a long hall was the sheriff's study. Alric had been there many times before, but always a constable escorted him.

He noted the fine tapestries and paintings on both sides along the length of the hallway. The castle was, throughout most of its interior, damp, dingy and cloaked in semi-darkness. How the sheriff could live here was a mystery to the undersheriff. The various wall hangings looked to Alric's untrained eye as if they needed attention. Not stopping to examine closer, the undersheriff was led through a double door into the sheriff's study.

The study was spacious with a warm fire burning on the far side of the room. Alric wondered at the need for such a fire at this time of year when the weather was warm and fair. However, he appreciated that it took the chill off the ancient stones of the castle walls.

The two walls opposite the grand fireplace contained floor-to-ceiling shelves loaded to straining with books, scrolls and documents of every kind including many legal tomes. Books were very expensive, especially a set of especially fine legal volumes that the undersheriff recognized after seeing a similar set at the abbey.

The undersheriff calculated that the sheriff must benefit from considerable wealth and wondered vaguely whence might be its source. In the centre of the room was a large oaken desk behind which the sheriff was sitting when Alric entered. The remaining wall bore a large set of doors leading out into the castle's courtyard. The doors through which the undersheriff entered were sheltered within one of the bookshelves.

"Welcome! Welcome! Master Alric! Thank you for coming so promptly! Have you yet supped?"

"No, Sir Henry. The message said urgent and here I am."

"Fine! Fine! Constable, find steward and tell him that cook needs to prepare some cakes and tea for the undersheriff. And tell him to tell her that I will be joining him. We will remain here, in the study."

"Now, Master Alric, to business before our repast arrives. I am pleased that you have captured that murderer Gilbert before he killed a third time. Well done, Master. Well done! But now we have another, perhaps more serious, issue with which we must deal."

"And that is, Sir?"

"The archdeacon."

"Why the archdeacon, Sir Henry? Surely, he knows of the murderer's crimes? What could he possibly want?"

"He wants, Master Alric, to try Gilbert in an ecclesiastical court."

"But that will never do, Sheriff. He has committed a hanging crime and if the jury finds him guilty, he must hang. The church will never hang him. We must resist this intrusion of the church into shire business, especially when the crime is so terrible." His voice rising, he pounded his fist on the sheriff's heavy oak desk.

"Now Master Alric. There is no need for that. We simply must get whatever help we need to negotiate with the archbishop. He certainly will not seek this himself. Oh no! He will call on his archdeacon, and it is with him you must negotiate."

"There is one who I believe can help us. He is a professor at Baliol. His name is Reginald Barrington. I believe that he is a friend of Lady Beatrix. She was helpful in solving the killings and bringing Gilbert before the bar. I believe I can persuade her to ask the professor to assist us.

The professor works at civil and canon law. He is an expert on heresy and church law and an interpreter of heretical symbols and texts."

"Forsooth, Master Alric! That certainly is the answer. See you to that immediately. The archbishop wants to send his archdeacon to us from his home church without delay. But now, our tea and cakes are here. Let us eat and then you can entreat Lady Beatrix for her assistance."

Alric – Negotiating with the Archdeacon

Undersheriff Alric, Sheriff Thisteldon, Archdeacon Edmund Lincoln, and Professor Reginald Barrington sat comfortably in the sheriff's study. Professor Barrington had been summoned by the lady Beatrix, and, in consideration of her family's generosity to Baliol College, he had agreed to meet.

The sheriff opened the conversation as the four men sipped their tea. "Professor, I am pleased that you were able to find time for us. You must be very busy, so we will not take too much of your time."

"When Lady Beatrix asked me to assist in the important discussion, I was pleased to do so. She and her family have been especially generous to the college, and this is the least I can do to demonstrate our appreciation."

The archdeacon clearly was uncomfortable. He was a big man, tall, with broad shoulders and a stern expression as he looked around at his three companions, imposing in his clerical garb.

"I must be clear, good sirs. This young man hath shown himself a most vile blasphemer and a dangerous heretic. Verily, he must not evade the church's chastisement."

Alric tensed at the archdeacon's firm declaration. "But, Archdeacon, this… this… Gilbert has committed murder. Not once, but twice, and has attempted yet a third, by God's grace unsuccessfully. He must face justice and receive his punishment!"

"But he hath blasphemed and called upon demons for aid. He hath invoked infernal names. His fate belongs to the church, not to your courts!"

The professor had been watching and listening silently. But now he spoke up in a low voice, calm and even. "Sheriff, Archdeacon, may I offer a suggestion, please? Truly, the church has a claim on this young man. There certainly are ample witnesses to his unholy outbursts. No doubt it will not be difficult to obtain a conviction and mete out the suitable punishment, likely excommunication.

"But suppose that, once your trial under canon law is complete, you were to release Master Gilbert into the undersheriff's custody? Master Alric can then imprison him to await civil trial. In this way both the church and the Crown may impose their respective forms of justice on the young man who so richly deserves it. As you imply, Archdeacon, his soul is forfeit. And in such state, his physical form, too, will perish."

More tea passed the lips of the four men, silently contemplating the professor's words. The archdeacon responded first. "That will be satisfactory for the church, kind sirs. Sheriff, can you agree to those terms?"

"Assuredly, Archdeacon. It is clear to me that our ends both may be served. Where will you try him?"

"Mayhap Saint Mary's will be suitable?"

"Satisfactory. We will make the arrangements to continue his incarceration in our dungeon until you send for him."

And, so the negotiation ended, more tea was consumed, and plans were laid.

Gilbert – A Trial Before God

Gilbert spent a difficult night in the castle's dungeon. It was a dark, dank place, with scant food and supplied with barely enough water to sustain him. He began screaming for a guard who never appeared.

When Gilbert was brought to the castle, he was deemed a particularly violent and dangerous prisoner. His two guards marched him down into the dungeons, past the common prison cells and farther down beneath St. George's Tower to an oubliette, a narrow, cramped, cold, damp pit accessible only from above.

One guard pinioned Gilbert's arms behind him while the other lifted the barred grate at the top of the cell. The two guards then hoisted him briefly and dropped him into the abyss. On the floor of the cell, barely able to move from the impact of the fall, Gilbert heard the grate slam shut above him, the bolt thrown and the guard's footsteps fading leaving him in dark, damp, cold silence.

Looking around in the dim light coming through the grate, Gilbert saw a pail of fetid water. There was no food in sight, and the cold, damp air made him shiver uncontrollably. He wrapped his cloak tighter around him hoping to ward off the cold and, exhausted, attempted to find sleep.

Sleep did not come to Gilbert that night, or for subsequent nights in the oubliette as he awaited trial. After a week in the pit, the guards came for him, pulled him from his cell and escorted him to the castle's interrogation chamber. There he saw a monk and a priest standing near to a rack intended to be used as a means of torture.

The priest spoke. "I am Father James, vicar general to the archdeacon of Lincoln."

"So, you intend to torture me, then." It was a statement, not a question.

"That depends upon your candour, Master Gilbert." It was the monk speaking. "I am Brother Ambrose once mentor to Thomas whom you brutally murdered. I shall count myself fortunate to hear your demented tale. And I am well-prepared to do what I must to hear that story." The monk's voice was icy cold. Gilbert could not believe that he was talking to a man who having taken the vows of a man of the cloth, threatened torture.

He began to be visibly nervous. The biting cold and bone-deep exhaustion that had consumed him now gave way to a growing fear. "What then, do you seek from me, Master... Monk?" Gilbert asked, his tone dripping with disdain.

Unruffled by the sarcasm, the monk responded with solemn gravity, "I seek to save your immortal soul, for though your body may perish from this life, your soul is eternal."

This struck Gilbert to his core. Rising to his full height, "It is you, Monk, who are the true blasphemer. I shall meet your lecturer in Hell as will I meet the father who withheld from me what is rightfully mine! I will meet them in Hell, Master Monk, and there will I murder them again, as I did the first time. They will die again under the benevolent gaze of Lord Saturn and all his demons who shall reward me for all eternity!"

His voice crescendoed as he cast his eyes and stretched his arms upward towards the chamber's high stone ceiling, breaking the iron grip of the two guards holding him. "Lord Saturn! Unleash all your demons upon this pretender who would dare to rip my soul from your fair and gentle embrace. Let him suffer tenfold the agony he intends for me. So shall it be decreed!"

Overwhelmed by his exertion and the weight of his own curse, Gilbert collapsed exhausted onto the cold stone floor.

The priest looked at the still form on the floor of the chamber, then to the monk. "It would appear, Brother that we have the confession we sought." Finally, to the guards, "Raise him up, guards, and take him to St. Mary's. There the archdeacon awaits."

The two guards half escorted, and half dragged Gilbert to the main level where they exited the castle and loaded Gilbert into a small, horse-drawn cart. With three guards walking on either side of the cart they drove through the crowds gathering along the way. When they arrived at St. Mary's Church in the heart of Oxford Town, the guards separated to keep the curious away from the prisoner while the remaining guards untied Gilbert's hands and dragged him through the great oak doors and into the nave of the church.

Still dragging their prisoner, the guards walked down the centre aisle of the nave and turned to enter the transept, a small area off the nave where people could sit in quiet contemplation or prayer. But there would be no quiet contemplation in the transept this day.

The archdeacon waited seated in his clerical robes behind a large, ornately carved desk brought in for the purpose of accommodating him. The guards jerked Gilbert awake. "Stand you straight and tall before the archdeacon, blasphemer. Archdeacon Lincoln, we have brought you the blasphemer, Gilbert of Shrewsbury."

"Has he confessed?"

"He has, Archdeacon."

"And have you the two required witnesses to his confession?"

"We do, Archdeacon."

Looking now at the priest, "And, what are the charges, pray tell?"

"He is charged with murder, blasphemy and heresy."

"Are the two required witnesses to his heresy and blaspheming present?"

From the priest, "We are, Archdeacon. The monk, Brother Ambrose, and I distinctly heard."

"How plead you, prisoner?" The archdeacon's voice was firm and his demeanour aloof.

Gilbert spat at the archdeacon, missing the voluminous vestments entirely. "You and your church be damned to Hell, preacher. I place my faith in Lord Saturn, not your puny God."

"Guards! Restrain the prisoner, bind his arms, and gag his blasphemous mouth!"

While one guard held Gilbert tightly with the point of his dagger at the prisoner's throat, the other guard bound his hands and applied the demanded gag.

"Now, witnesses, describe his rantings that require that you present him here for judgement by the holy church."

The monk and priest described the episode in the interrogation chamber of the castle. The archdeacon thought for a moment, "I see. Well, his behaviour today mimics his behaviour at the castle, so I have no choice but to rule for conviction."

Turning to the prisoner, the prelate intoned a prayer in Latin. "*Omnipotens Pater, qui omnium hominum iudex es, te rogamus ut hoc coetum tua sapientia divina dirigas. Da nobis fortitudinem tuam iustitiam cum misericordia exercere, et sanctitatem mandatorum tuorum custodire. Fac ut nostra acta voluntatem tuam reflectant, et ad pacem et iustitiam in communitate nostra afferendam operentur. Misericordiam tuam de anima accusati petimus, ut in tua divina gratia redemptionem inveniat.* Amen"

Turning to the assembled onlookers, "For those who labor in the tongue of our land, Almighty Father, who art the judge of all mankind, we beseech thee to guide this assembly with thy divine wisdom. Grant us the strength to enact thy justice with mercy and to uphold the sanctity of thy commandments. May our actions reflect thy will, and may they serve to bring peace and righteousness to our community. We ask for thy mercy on the soul of the accused, that he may find redemption in thy divine grace. Amen"

The archdeacon then, rose from his chair, his robes rustling slightly in the silence of the great cathedral, his lips compressed and his eyes hard, addressed the prisoner: "*Nos, auctoritate nobis commissa, te, Gilbertum, reum invenimus criminum quae contra te citata sunt. Propter haec, tibi poenam dignam pronuntiamus.*

By the authority vested in us, we find you, Gilbert, guilty of the crimes charged against you. For these, we pronounce upon you the deserved punishment."

Pausing, "Remove the gag and bindings from the prisoner, guards. He must be free to accept his punishment. But do you keep a close watch.

Pro gravitate scelerum tuorum, quae ecclesiam nostram maculant, te, Gilbertum, anathemate condemnamus. Excommunicamus et anathematizamus te, et a liminibus sanctae matris ecclesiae separamus, donec ad poenitentiam revertearis.

Given the gravity of your sins, which defile our church, we therefore condemn you, Gilbert, with anathema. We excommunicate and anathematize you and separate you from the thresholds of the holy mother church, until you return to penitence."

Gilbert's response was immediate. Struggling against the iron hold of the guards, with a howl he lunged toward the archdeacon, his hands clawing through the air for the archdeacon's throat. Instantly, one of the guards extended his staff to bar the prisoner's path. Tripping over the extended staff, Gilbert fell against the floor of the church before he could make good his attack, his head striking the hard, stone floor.

The archdeacon, his expression grim but controlled, watched without flinching. "Guards, remove the prisoner from our sacred church and see to his wounds. He has been tried before God. Now, return him to the dungeons to await his trial before man."

Gilbert – The End of The Road

The sheriff and the undersheriff were in the castle with Professor Reginald Barrington. Up in the grand hall, surrounded by large portraits of sheriffs and castellans from days gone by, lavish tapestries, and arms of several noble families, the three talked over wine and bread. The Sheriff, Sir Henry, seemed to be the controlling voice. "Well, we must wait for the Assizes, next here in a fortnight. In the meanwhile, I will gather two juries from the local hundred, taking care to include only freemen and those who have served on juries in the past."

The professor was thoughtful. "It is important that your jury understand the gravity of Gilbert's crimes without being unable to judge fairly. It were best if you avoided people who knew either Gilbert or the victims. We don't know, of course, who the Crown's judge will be, but you may be assured that he will be a knowledgeable, thorough and fair jurist. I will undertake to represent the Crown. Does the prisoner have an advocate?"

"No, professor." The undersheriff mulled over the problem. "Without his representative he may not be able to raise a convincing defence."

"I would not be too concerned about that, though. He likely will attempt to defend himself, but, logically, he really has no defence. Why, he damned himself with his own words!"

The sheriff spoke up, "Master Undersheriff, please see to it that the prisoner knows that he is entitled to counsel. Ask him if there is someone for whom you should send."

"Aye Sheriff. I will see to that myself. It is too important to delegate it.

"Thank you, Master Alric. I will see to it, with the professor's kind assistance, that the prisoner and the Crown are ready for the presentment. Professor, you will, I trust, address the court yourself?"

"Indeed, Lord Sheriff. I shall present the case for judgement as to whether it is ripe for the trial jury. The presentment court will, I am certain however, bind Master

Gilbert over for jury trial."

"Very well, then." The sheriff rose from his chair signaling that the conversation was at an end. "We shall meet again before the presentment to ensure that we have all that we need to obtain, ultimately, a conviction."

A week later, the crown judge and his retinue had arrived and were comfortably ensconced in luxurious quarters within the castle. The two trials–presentment and, if necessary, the jury trial–were to be held in the great hall. Servants had already prepared the place of the trial for the jury, judge, advocates, and the prisoner.

At the appointed time two guards escorted the prisoner to a heavy chair. He was shackled to prevent escape or violence and was attended by three burly guards, one behind him and one on either side of the chair. The judge for the Crown ascended a small, raised dais and was seated in a large ornate chair, almost resembling a throne.

On benches facing the judge sat the jury of twelve men, selected for their status and, in some few cases, their occupations. There was a large, plain, oaken table behind which the sheriff, undersheriff and the professor sat surrounded by stacks of notes on parchment. There were several benches arranged for spectators, for this trial was the talk of Oxford Town since it was announced that the killer had been apprehended.

The witnesses, including Brother Ambrose, the deputy coroner, the priest who had witnessed Gilbert's outburst, and Lady Beatrix speaking for herself and Sister Agnes, still at the abbey, joined the three men at the large, heavy table. Standing quietly in the corner of the large, high-ceilinged room was a constable with his arbalest.

The judge turned to the jury. "Are you ready to proceed?"

A man, clearly of noble birth, judging by his rich tunic trimmed at the neck and cuffs in ermine, rose, "We are my Lord."

"And the case for the Crown?" The Professor stood facing the magistrate, "Aye, my lord. Quite prepared."

"Very well, then, let us begin. It is Professor Barrington, is it not?"

"Aye, my lord. And we have met before, have we not?"

"Indeed, we have, Professor. Are you acting as the King's Advocate in this case?"

"I am. I am supported by the sheriff and undersheriff of Oxfordshire."

"Good. Good. Proceed, then, Professor."

"My Lord, today we bring you the case of Master Gilbert of Shrewsbury, accused of two murders and one attempted murder. Additionally, he has been accused by the Holy Roman Church of the most egregious blasphemy and heresy. The Church found him guilty and subjected him to anathema and excommunication. We will call Undersheriff Alric the Bald to describe the crimes.

Master Undersheriff, please describe the crimes that you have investigated that you believe were committed by the accused."

The undersheriff rose and faced the jurors. "As will be outlined in the coroner's rolls, the accused murdered, wilfully and with malice aforethought one Thomas of Hereford, lecturer at Baliol College. Master Thomas was dispatched outside the walls of Rewley Abbey by means of a long sharp blade.

Additionally, the accused murdered, wilfully and with malice aforethought, his own father, Master Edmund of Shrewsbury in his butcher shop here in Oxford Town. The accused dispatched his father using a heavy mallet, delivering several blows to his father's head."

"His own father, Professor? How can this be?" The judge was incredulous. "This is among the worst and most vile of crimes. Have you a witness?"

"There is no witness to the killing My Lord, however, there are two witnesses who heard him confess to both murders."

"This is heinous! Please call your witnesses, Professor."

"My Lord, I first will call the deputy coroner, Adam de Wallingford. Deputy Coroner, did you convene inquests into these two deaths?"

"I did, Professor."

"And what was their outcome?"

"With the assistance of Sister Agnes, infirmarist at the convent, we determined cause and manner of death in both cases."

"And is Sister Agnes present, Professor?" The judge leaned slightly forward in his chair, his judicial robes reaching almost to the floor of the dais.

"No, My Lord. She does not leave the convent. However, she works closely with Lady Beatrix de Aylesbridge, a lady of noble birth and the eldest child of an old and respected family. She was present at the postmortem examinations of the victims, and, in fact, assisted Sister Agnes. She testified at both coroner's inquests on her own and Sister Agnes' behalf."

"And is Lady Beatrix present today?"

"She is. May I call her for her testimony?"

"Please do, Professor."

"Lady Beatrix. Thank you for attending us on this day, my lady. Briefly what were your findings in your, and

Sister Agnes' examination of the two victims?"

"Our findings, Professor, are outlined in detail in Sister Agnes' written reports. I will summarize. The two victims were killed as you described. However, it was clear that the killer enacted both attacks in fits of rage. This was shown by the ferocity of the attacks and the fact that they both were delt many more blows than necessary to kill them."

"I have read the reports, Lady Beatrix. They are remarkable for their detail, conclusions, and completeness. Professor, do you then submit these reports along with the coroner's rolls as evidence?"

"I do, my lord."

"Very well. Scribe, collect these reports and provide them to the jury."

"Aye, m'lord."

"And have you more for us, Professor?"

"Just one thing, my lord. There are two witnesses to the accused's confession."

"Call the first of your witnesses."

"Thank you, my lord. I call the priest, Father James, vicar general to the archdeacon of Lincoln, who was present when the accused was questioned prior to his ecclesiastical trial. Father, did you, with your own ears, and being present at the time hear the confession of the accused?"

"I did, Professor."

"And can you repeat that confession?"

"I can. Never shall I forget his terrible words. He stood, looked at me straight on with a look that will haunt my dreams forever. He then turned to the monk who was with us. His words were:

'It is you, Monk, who are the true blasphemer. I shall

meet your lecturer in Hell as will I meet the father who withheld from me what is rightfully mine! I will meet them in Hell, Master Monk, and there will I murder them again, as I did the first time. They will die again under the benevolent gaze of Lord Saturn and all his demons who shall reward me for all eternity!'

He was addressing Brother Ambrose, a Cistercian monk from Rewley Abby who was there at the questioning."

"And is Brother Ambrose here today, Professor?"

"He is my lord. Brother Ambrose also is the one who discovered the lecturer's body outside the abbey walls."

"Rewley Abbey, Professor?"

"Yes, my lord."

"Is all this true as you recall, Brother?"

"It is my lord. Exactly as I recall."

"Professor, have you any more for us?"

"No, my lord. Nothing more."

"I should think that we need no more to tell this terrible story. Master Forman, does the jury wish to confer before issuing a finding?"

The nobleman leaned toward his fellow jurors who whispered to one another for a few short moments before he turned back to the Judge. "My lord, we need no further time to debate the outcome of this presentment. We find, and so say we each and so say we all, that we must bind the accused over for jury trial."

Time seemed to stop in the grand hall where the court was assembled as Gilbert, with the apparent strength of ten men, threw off his guards, sending them sprawling to the castle floor. With a mighty roar, holding his arms out in front of him, his shackles poised in front of him to strangle the judge.

At once he seemed taller and stronger than the meek, exhausted prisoner he had been. No longer was his visage a pasty white. No longer was he so weak that he hardly could stand. He kicked the heavy chair in which he was sitting behind him, raised his eyes to the ceiling of the great hall and shouted in a voice that shook the walls of the room.

"You, Master Judge, shall NOT judge ME! I do not accept your court or your puny God. I place my soul in the gentle keeping of Lord Saturn. He shall be my rock and he shall guide my vengeful hands to your scrawny throat!"

Gilbert was nearly at the feet of the dais, his eyes bulging wildly, grasping for the judge who had stood and fearfully started to back away from the prisoner who now seemed a monster from Hell bent upon revenge. "I shall never see a jury trial because YOU, Master Judge, will NOT BE HERE TO CONDUCT IT!"

As he was reaching over the final few feet to the judge, the constable in the corner raised his arbalest and fired. The bolt found its mark in Gilbert's throat, but the raging prisoner was not stopped in his quest for the judge and his violent vengeance.

Before the constable could recharge his weapon, one of the guards, thrown aside by the prisoner in his wild escape, rose from the floor where he had fallen, drew his sword and buried its blade in Gilbert's chest. The prisoner shuddered and stalled in his attack against the judge. A second guard stood and with a mighty swing of his heavy broadsword at the prisoner's neck, severed his head from his body.

It was over.

The terror that had enveloped the court and, indeed, all of Oxford Town with its violent villainy, was lying harmless on the stone floor, his severed head, eyes wide and mouth gaping in its final curse, beside him where it had fallen.

CHAPTER 22: THE CHILLING EVE

In which a chilling discovery after evening prayers leads Sister Agnes to question the extent of malevolent forces at play as she uncovers a missing fragment of a manuscript, hinting at sinister undercurrents that may threaten the peace of Godstow Abbey.

It had been several weeks since the dramatic death of Gilbert, the Killer. The superstitious in the town grumbled about hauntings and more killings by Gilbert's shade. The more educated worried that those who feared the repercussions of one associated with demons and spirits would disrupt the usual peace of the university town.

The town fathers, responding to these concerns and fears, burned Gilbert's body to ashes in a public square. The ashes were divided amongst four knights from the small local troop of Templars.

As the Templars mounted their huge white war horses, battle armor on horse and man gleaming in the bright sunlight, each knight held a leathern pouch containing part of Gilbert's ashes. The eldest knight, Sir Gadwin, raised his pouch high before the crowd, his voice carrying over the murmurs.

"Now, before God and our brethren, we cast away the darkness that has lingered over Oxford Town. To the north, south, east, and west, these ashes shall be scattered to the winds."

The crowd, fearful peasants, curious scholars from the university, and weary town officials, watched the knights ride out. It was a dramatic spectacle to unite and fortify them.

Before long, tales of the knights' journeys far past the ends of the town's boundaries became interwoven with the fabric of local lore, Gilbert's reign of terror faded into a tale of knightly heroism that would be told to generations of Oxford's children.

Isabel – The Future

The summons was simple yet authoritative. Another novice came to Isabel in her chamber shortly before Vespers. "You must away with me Sister. Mother has summoned you and we must not keep her waiting." Isabel's day of reckoning had arrived.

Together the novices went to the abbess' parlour, somewhat more sumptuous than her spartan chamber. It was here, in this pleasant room, that Mother met with visitors, dignitaries, benefactors and, occasionally, members of the community with whom she wished an important, private discussion.

Isabel, eyes filled with tears and her hands trembling with fear, entered the room. Her escort did not follow her past the large oaken double doors. She looked about the room with its beautiful stained-glass window looking out over the gardens. On the walls was a large, but plain, crucifix and tapestries and paintings depicting various religious scenes. Isabel was engrossed in these, perhaps wishing that she could dissolve into one of the tapestries and be away from the abbey protected by the angels she saw on the hanging. The escort quietly closed the doors.

"Sister Isabel…" it was Mother summoning her. With

her was sister Agnes. Isabel knelt at the ornate prie-dieu facing Mother and Sister Agnes awaiting what she was certain would be a harsh judgement.

Both nuns wore grave, but not hostile expressions. Mother Alice began, "Sister, you have sinned gravely, but you did what you felt that you must. This is what happens when we listen to the words of man rather than the words of God. You have much to learn and, with God's help you will, in time, learn and grow. In the meantime, you may remain here as a novice. When your one-year penance is complete we will decide haw the proceed."

Then it was Sister Agnes' turn. "Sister, your penance dictates that half of your day be spent in prayer and contemplation. The other half is to be passed continuing to do your usual tasks. That means that you will continue to assist me in the infirmary. I will, with Mother's help and God's guidance, be your spiritual guide and counsellor."

Mother Alice, "Do you understand, Sister?"

"Yes, Mother. Bless you for your understanding."

"Oh, I do understand, Sister. But that does not mean that I approve."

"I understand, Mother."

"Now, we must away to Vespers and supper."

Sister Agnes
– A Revelation Threatens the Peace of The Abbey

Vespers were over and Sister Agnes was finding it difficult to eat. The meeting with Mother and Isabel lay heavy upon her. She knew that the penance was fair. In fact, anything short of excommunication was fair under the circumstances. Leaving her sisters at their meals, Agnes returned to her workroom.

She stood by her worktable gazing idly about the room where she had healed so many of her sisters and lost a few as well. It was where she performed postmortem examinations of the victims of Gilbert the Killer. She shuddered involuntarily at the recollection. That, thanks to Jesus, Mary and all the blessed saints was over, now only a sad and unpleasant memory slowing fading into the dim mists of the past.

As she turned her gaze upon her personal books and parchments – a small but special library that helped her access the healing arts – something seemed wrong. It was as if someone had pawed through the collection. She knew that she would never treat her precious library thus and she was quite sure that Isabel would treat the volumes as gently as she herself would. But still…

Agnes browsed the little library with increasing intensity. Something certainly was wrong, but she simply could not see what it was. Then, suddenly, she saw.

Her fragment of the Picatrix, an 11th century treatise on astrological magic containing arcane, occult knowledge had been moved from it from its usual resting place. She did not possess the entire book. The knowledge it contained was heretical and blasphemous. Such occult lore had no place in the abbey. She was careful about possessing such books and manuscripts.

Thus, she owned but a single part of *The Picatrix:* Book 4 Chapter 7, a chapter from "The things in the magical art found in the book *The Chaldean Agriculture* which Abudaer Abmiaxie translated from the Chaldean Language into Arabic". Agnes had obtained a Latin translation from an itinerant monk returning from the Holy Land to his monastery in a nearby shire. This chapter contained many useful potions that Agnes used both in her healing arts and in maintaining her herb garden. However, it also contained a section on "Deadly Poisons."

With trembling hands Agnes removed the book from the shelf and started to page slowly through it. The sections "A Deadly Poison" and "Another Deadly Poison" had been roughly torn from the volume. She browsed further and found that another section, one which she had referred to in the past, "A Theriac for Every Poison" was, likewise, missing. This was a cure for all types of poisoning.

Someone, clearly, was acting out a poisoning ritual and, not wishing to take unnecessary chances, took the formula for the antidote as well. *But who in the abbey would do such an unholy thing?* Sister Agnes could not imagine it of one of her sisters.

Both poisons needed to be administered by painting the point of a knife or spear with them. That suggested the nuns who worked in the kitchen with their sharp knives.

She replaced what was left of the manuscript and left the workroom. Still pondering her lost manuscript pages, it occurred to her that a gardener who also used sharp tools from time to time was likewise a possibility. Who, besides herself could that possibly be? Then, with a flash the answer came:

Isabel!

HISTORICAL NOTES

Many of the medieval locations and streets in Oxford Town no longer exist in modern Oxford. Both Rewley Abbey and Godstow Abby have been reduced to ruins over the centuries, but those ruins are available to visit today. This street map is the most recent depiction of early Oxford streets that I could find.

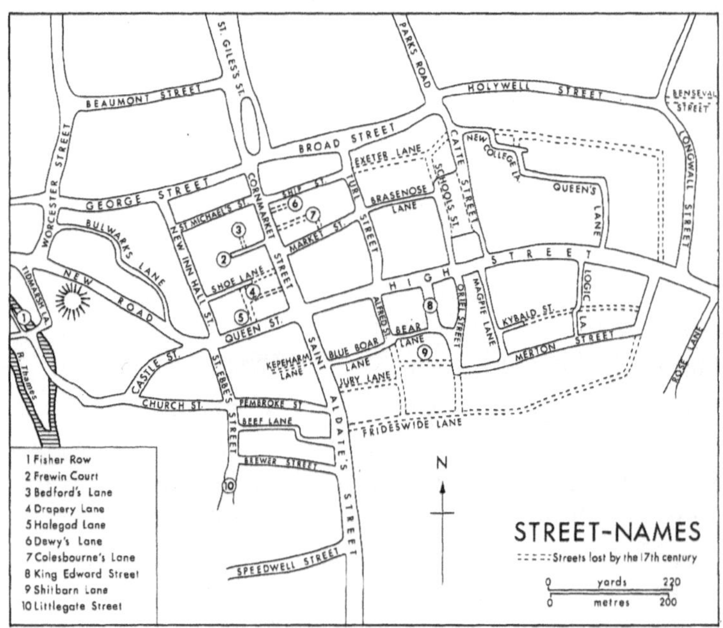

Most of the characters are fictitious, however, I did evoke the shades of some historical figures.

Mother Alice de Gorges was the Mother Superior/Abbess of Godstow from 1285 to 1304. Lady Rosamunde de Clifford–"The Fair Rosamunde"–was the mistress of Henry II. She was buried upon her death within the walls of Godstow Abbey. However, in 1190, Bishop Hugh of Lincoln ordered that she be re-buried outside of the hallowed grounds of the abbey.

Adam de Spaulding was the actual coroner for Oxford during the period of this story. However, to avoid placing him in positions that were not historically accurate, I gave him a fictitious deputy coroner. I did much the same with the actual historical sheriff, Henry de Thistledon. I gave him a fictitious undersheriff, Alric the Bald. However, in the closing scenes of the story I allowed the good sheriff his place in footlights. Those scenes are completely fictitious.

Alexis the Bard of the Shire is a fictional character. However, she is based upon a real young lady, a singer/songwriter in the Detroit, Michigan area. She is incredibly talented and a real "up-and-comer" in the area. As far as I know, the real Alexis does not have "the sight" as claims our bard.

During the Middle Ages, superstition among the uneducated classes was rampant. I have alluded to that in several places. However, the most egregious example of a fraud taking advantage of the "masses" in our story was in the person of Wystan the Sage.

By manipulating hallucinogenic drugs which he burnt as incense, he was able to convince people that he was performing, with the help of his demons, real magic spells. His fraud perpetrated against Gilbert probably started him on his downward spiral to insanity, and, ultimately, his death.

Wystan, though not a genuine historical character, was typical of the "sorcerers" who roamed medieval England and Europe running their scams against gullible people.

The rituals at the abbey and, in general, of the Catholic Church, which retained power in England until the time of Henry VIII, are abbreviated versions – to make it a bit less tedious for the reader – of actual rituals of the time. I have used Latin, the language of the church, sparingly, for realism, and, when I have used it, the scene contains English translations.

The procedures for the trials and coroner's inquest are taken from examples of actual trial as well as the coroner's rolls of the period.

With those exceptions, all of the story is fiction and, as they say, any resemblance to actual persons, living or dead, is coincidental.

--Dr. Peter Stephenson

ACKNOWLEDGEMENTS

At the top of my list are my son and daughter, especially my daughter, who interrupted her busy legal practice to be a beta reader.

A special acknowledgement goes to Dee Marley who edited the book… I have been writing in various genre for almost 50 years and this is undoubtedly the best editing I ever have seen. Thank you, Ms Marley!!

Thank you to Ms Sunny Bleau, a popular blues artist in the Detroit, Michigan area, for being a beta reader even though she had to fit reading the draft in with her busy tour schedule. I imagine much reading was on her tour bus on the way to her next gig.

I long have railed against Facebook as being empty-headed entertainment for people with empty heads. Mea culpa!! I repent having ever held that opinion. Two Facebook groups provided expert advice over the writing of this story: the History of Oxford and the Historical Fiction Club. To those who straightened me out when I was in error, eternal thanks!

Of course there have been several beta readers, too many to call out here, but you know who you are, and my sincere thanks!

Finally, but certainly not the least of these acknowledgements, I must thank one who kept me on schedule by coming into my study every other week to ask if I was finished yet. The delightful lady who keeps my house ship-shape made sure that the story was moving along because she wanted to read it.

So, to my publishers: including my immediate family and others who have kept me going, we have half a dozen sales. The rest, my friends, are up to you.

--Dr. Peter Stephenson

Preview: Book 2 of the Sister Agnes and Lady Beatrix Mysteries – <u>The Witch of Godstow Abbey</u>

Introduction

It had been an especially warm Autumn following close on the heels of a hot Spring and Summer in 1299 Oxford Town. Kneeling in the dirt of the infirmary's herb garden, Sister Agnes, and her novice Isabel, were hurrying to get the wintering-over herbs in the ground, assuring a fresh supply when Spring 1300 arrived. Agnes, as the infirmarist of Godstow Abbey, saw to the growing and harvesting of the herbs to be used as healing potions.

Garlic, sage, chamomile, calendula, and foxglove all were important for Agnes' collection of herbs for her infirmary. As she prepared the soft earth to receive her plantings, she meditated on some of her herbs. Foxglove was very important. Used to treat her older nuns who had illnesses of the heart, this drug needed to be used with care. Calendula Agnes used on rashes of the skin. As she dug, she prayed to various saints who would help her seeds grow into healthy herb plants to be harvested for her workroom.

Saint Fiacre was the patron saint of gardeners and herbalists. Hildegard of Bingen was a Benedictine abbess known for her expertise as an herbalist. And, of course, she could not complete her garden without a prayer to St. Benedict, the patron Saint of her order of Benedictine nuns.

The autumn sun was starting to set, signalling that it was time to leave the garden, perform their ablutions and go to the chapel for Vespers, when Isabel, from the other side of the garden screamed loudly, over and over with urgent cries of "Sister, Sister, come quickly!" in between.

"What on earth is it, child? Are you injured?"

Isabel was breathless. "N… n… no, Sister. But you must c… c… come. Hurry!" And the panicked screaming began anew.

Agnes walked rapidly around to the other side where Isabel was on her hands and knees, a garden claw waving wildly in her hand. There on the ground in front of Isabel, half buried in the soft freshly turned earth, were three tiny bodies.

And so, our story begins.

== *0* ==

www.historiumpress.com